A ROOM ON THE MOUNTAIN

Also by this author

Biography
Susanna Moodie: Pioneer Author (2006)

Poetry
An Angel around the Corner/ Un ange autour du coin
(2004)
All We Need/ Tout ce qu'il faut (2002)
No Country for Women(1993)

Fiction & Poems
A Skin of Snow(1981)

A ROOM ON THE MOUNTAIN

A Novella

By

Anne Cimon

GEMMA BOOKS

Author photo by Munira Judith Avinger

ISBN 978-0-9690747-1-7

GEMMA BOOKS
Greenfield Park, QC
Canada

Acknowledgments

I am grateful to the Writers' Trust of Canada's Woodcock Fund for a grant to complete this work.

I thank Munira Judith Avinger for being my "writing buddy" through the years and for her major contribution in editing and revising the manuscript of this book with great patience, sensitivity, and good humour.

I also want to thank family and friends who encourage and support me in my work. Your care and nurture of the artist in me means so much.

"The person undergoing an operative procedure experiences an unusually intense sense of *rescue* thanks to the power that the surgeon wields. The physical proximity between the two also brings with it extreme *intimacy*."

Richard Horton, *Health Wars*

IN THE HOSPITAL

At eight a.m., while other people prepared to go to work, Caroline scrubbed herself with a disinfectant soap, in a dirty shower stall, on the nineteenth floor of the Mountainside Hospital. She didn't want to take a shower but she had to for the operation.

"I don't know if I'm ready," she'd told the surgeon, Dr. Pine, on the phone. She was considering letting herself die rather than face the operation. The biggest worry was how could she survive this ordeal without Thomas, her husband, by her side? He'd passed away in the same hospital two years before.

"Mrs. Sauvé, "Dr. Pine replied, "You might not live if you wait too long."

She had thought it was harsh of him to suggest she could die but it did have the desired effect. He scared her enough that she agreed he could set the date for the operation. And now this was the day. Caroline lathered her hair with her own shampoo which she'd been allowed to use. Her dark roots were showing since she hadn't had the time, or the inclination, to go to the hairdresser for the blond colour. When sick, you let go of artifice.

She remembered what the nurse had said in the pre-op *spiel*:

"Now don't bother painting your toenails pretty for the doctor, you'll have to take the polish off for the operation."

The nurse laughed but Caroline didn't, that infernal day when she'd run the gamut of pre-op tests. She remembered how touched she'd been that her friend Joanie, who accompanied her, had supplied a snack of apple juice and homemade cookies.

Caroline's toenails were now bare of colour, and her hair needed colour, but what she wanted most was to come out of the hospital feeling her old self again. No one could guarantee the operation would be a success, not even her surgeon. The pre-op nurse commented:

"Oh, Dr. Pine, he is very meticulous, he takes time with each operation."

That made Caroline feel worse because it would mean she would be under the anesthetic longer, and she knew the toll this took on body and mind.

In the shower room, Caroline looked for a plug for her hairdryer. She saw one by the mirror above the sink, but when she tried it, it didn't work. She'd left the door open and noticed the nurse Carmella walk by. She called out: "This plug doesn't work." Her hair wet, Caroline was shivering despite the warmth of her bathrobe. Carmella smiled at her. She was half her age, probably twenty-five, tall and big-boned. She wore a pixie haircut and had an intelligent, caring gaze.

"Be careful, you could get electrocuted, there is water all over the floor."

It was true, her feet were in a puddle, but Caroline didn't care. It might be less painful to be electrocuted than to endure the surgery.

"You'll have to use the plug by your bed," Carmella said.

"I don't want to disturb anyone with the noise."

Caroline worried about the other patients. The hairdryer was loud and she knew that Mr. Pinto, in the bed next to her, needed his rest.

"There is no other plug," Carmella said in a nurse's matter-of-fact tone. She led the way back to the ward. Caroline's bed was situated by the window and she had a panoramic view of the city, the St-Lawrence River and the South Shore, where she continued to live in the apartment she'd shared with Thomas. Their cat Mel was being cared for by a neighbour she could trust. Caroline noticed how the leaves on the trees were that bitter green of late summer before they change to the brilliant gold of fall.

The drapes were pulled around Mr. Pinto's bed. She knew Nina, his wife, was sitting with him, just as Thomas would be sitting by her bed if he were alive, and just as she had been with him when he was dying. She plugged her hairdryer in and the loud noise started. "I'm so sorry," she mouthed towards Mrs. Coffey who lay propped up by several pillows in a bed across the room. She'd had open heart surgery. Her daughter sat on a metal chair beside her.

Caroline waved the hairdryer around her head as fast as she could. Her hair wasn't as thick as it used to be due to the years of stresses and illnesses, both her own and Thomas. She heard a groan from behind the curtain. Poor Mr. Pinto had emergency surgery, and she'd heard him ask in his delirium during the night:

"Why did they do this to me?"

His wife had answered softly:

"You were having a heart attack, Gino; they had to do this to save your life."

13

Caroline knew what he meant though. Why does anyone have to go through such suffering? What was the sense of it?

* * *

The operation was scheduled for eleven thirty. Caroline had three more hours to wait and she knew surgeries were sometimes delayed. What could she do to fill the time?

She sat in the blue armchair, in the narrow space between her bed and the window, and stared at the view. Wealthy people bought mansions on Mount Royal for the same breathtaking sight of city skyline, river, and mountain range beyond. She noticed a Canadian flag and Quebec flag flying side by side on the roof of a brownstone building across the avenue. She liked to see how the flags were blown together by the breeze.

Her breathing was difficult due to the exertion of drying her hair and the anxiety she was feeling. Caroline didn't want to think of all the tubes she would be waking up with. The afternoon before had been crazy. She'd sat in this chair in her street clothes; loathe to change into the pale blue hospital gown that had been provided for her.

Joanie had accompanied her through the admission process and agreed to stay a bit longer. She perched herself on the edge of the bed, a reassuring presence.

They were surprised when Dr. Pine appeared before them. Neither had heard him enter the room. He wasn't wearing his white lab coat, but a dark suit and tie, as if he were going to a conference or a banquet dinner.

"Mrs. Sauvé, how are you? Are you ready for tomorrow's surgery?"

Caroline looked at the man standing a few feet from her. She felt uncomfortable at the thought that he would be the one to operate. He was a young surgeon with not a grey hair in sight. Did he know what he was doing? Dr. Pine possessed a smooth face like a model in a men's fragrance ad. Caroline wasn't sure if she liked him or not as he seemed a bit fresh in his manner. The question about being ready for the operation had been rhetorical, since Dr. Pine continued:

"I must tell you that there is always a risk in such an operation. The procedure is generally successful but there is always a chance to provoke a heart attack or a stroke. This is very rare."

Caroline was getting more and more upset. She didn't remember Dr. Pine telling her this but perhaps she had blocked it out. Had he tricked her into the whole thing? What did he mean? Couldn't he tell the outcome from all the tests and scans she'd suffered through?

"Well, I don't want this operation if you can't guarantee I will come out of it okay."

Dr. Pine pressed his lips together in displeasure at her reaction:

"Mrs Sauvé, there is only a small chance of that. Have confidence in me."

This last phrase he liked to repeat often, but why should she have confidence in him? She looked at Joanie:

"What do you think?"

"Well, the odds are good."

That was true. She trusted Joanie. And what was she to do? Un-admit herself from the hospital? She was way too exhausted for that.

"Okay then."

Dr. Pine smiled. She couldn't smile back. She wanted to crawl under the bed like her cat when it was frightened. It was taking all her strength to even talk.

Dr. Pine said a polite goodbye and left as quickly as he'd arrived.

Now as Caroline sat in the blue armchair by her bed, she imagined him scrubbing for his first operation of the morning. One thing she'd noticed was how clean and well-manicured Dr. Pine's hands were, the fingernails buffed. Thomas had suspected his specialist, Dr. Jurgen, hadn't washed his hands between patients since he'd often fallen ill after a check-up. Caroline had recently seen Dr. Jurgen in the hospital corridor. He stood out since he was six feet tall with a white beard and a paunch like Santa. He'd turned red and pretended he didn't see her. Perhaps he was still upset by the loss of Thomas. She didn't want to mull over that. She was weak from fasting for her operation.

The ward was eerily tranquil. Mr. Pinto was resting behind the curtain while Nina went to the cafeteria. Mrs. Coffey slept, the sheet pulled up to her chin. She moaned from time to time. Her recovery wasn't easy. Pat, her daughter was there by her side. "Hi, mum," she'd whispered, when she entered the room at dawn. "It's Pat. I'll just sit beside you. Keep resting."

Caroline wished she wasn't alone. She was disappointed that her sister Paulina couldn't take the day off from the clinic where she worked but she promised to be there in the evening after the operation. Caroline felt panic rise in her. She had to get out of the room. As she walked by Mrs. Coffey's bed, she blurted out to Pat:

"I'm having an operation this morning."

Caroline had learned over the years that telling strangers your story relieved some anxiety. She'd been shy as a child, sometimes unable to finish her sentences. A psychotherapist had helped her to speak out and find her own voice.

Pat turned all her attention on Caroline who guessed that she must look awful. "Why don't we take a walk down the hall together?" Pat suggested. Caroline was touched that she would want to leave her mother's bedside to accompany her.

The hall was bright with the morning sunshine, and busy with bustling nurses and orderlies. They had to watch out for the carts of breakfast trays, the stretchers, the buckets. Pat stayed close. She told her she had driven in from the Townships. She was shorter than Caroline and wore beige pants and a white blouse.

"My husband died two years ago in this hospital."

"I'm sorry for your loss," Pat answered in a sincere tone.

"I'm so nervous about the operation," Caroline added.

"That's normal," Pat said. "I'm sure it will go well for you." Her positive words comforted Caroline.

"Whatever happens, you'll be able to cope," Pat offered. "You'll recover quickly, you're young. And you're pretty and could remarry."

Caroline knew she looked young but she would be in the hospital for her fiftieth birthday. And would she remarry?

They reached the end of the hall. No doubt Pat was worried about her mother. Caroline said she felt better and wanted to return to the room. As she entered, before she had time to reach her bed, an orderly rolled in a gurney:

"Mrs. Sauvé?"

"Oui," Caroline answered. She reverted to her mother tongue when she was stressed.

"They are ready for you downstairs," he announced.

She couldn't believe it. It wasn't even eleven o'clock. They had come for her early. Bless Dr. Pine. Perhaps he had taken pity on her. Had he bumped another patient for her? Caroline felt relief that the wait was over and lay down on the gurney. She had to be brave and do what she was told.

"Good luck!" Pat said when Caroline was rolled out of the room.

* * *

The orderly pushed the gurney down the hall past the nursing station. Caroline thought she saw some nurses wave at her. The tranquilizer she'd been given was beginning to make her drowsy. The orderly stopped at the elevators and waited for the one that would take them to the surgery floor. The door opened with a clang. Luckily it was empty. Caroline didn't like being in a confined space like an elevator. But she was now more in a panic about how she would be anesthesized.

"We're going to have to put a tube down your throat while you are still awake," Dr. Lope, the chief anesthesiologist had insisted during the pre-op appointment. He had told her to open her mouth and place two fingers inside. She didn't like to do this, but she knew that in the hospital, you had to do things, whether you liked it or not.

Dr. Lope said he wanted to gauge how wide the passage was for the tube.

"I don't want a tube down my throat while I'm awake."

That seemed the most terrifying thing that could be done to her. Dr. Lope stiffened at her statement, his bloodshot eyes widening. There was something unhealthy about him. His skin was yellow and taunt as if he suffered from jaundice.

"We cannot take any chance that you choke when you are anesthesized."

"I will ask Dr. Pine about this," Caroline said. She could see that this doctor really didn't like that she talked back to him. He looked angry. She felt like calling the whole operation off. Later that afternoon, back at home, Caroline dialled Dr. Pine's office. To her surprise, she was able to reach him. He reassured her he would talk to Dr. Lope about the tube. But had he?

The elevator door opened and the orderly, who was silent throughout the ride down, wheeled her into a dark hallway. He stopped and left the gurney by a set of swinging doors that resembled those in a country & western bar.

"You won't have to wait long," he said, then walked away. Two young men in green scrubs pushed through the swinging doors:

"Are you Mrs. Sauvé?" the taller one asked.

"Oui," Caroline answered.

"I'm Dr. Rossi. I will be your anesthesiologist. This is my assistant, Dr. Clark."

He waved at the shorter man beside him. She nodded, relieved that Dr. Lope wasn't mentioned. "I'm scared," she said. This had become her mantra. It helped to say it out loud.

"Yes, we understand. It's normal." Dr. Rossi said.

"I was told that a tube might be put down my throat while I am awake." Caroline ventured. "I don't want that at all."

Would they think she was a difficult patient? So what? She read somewhere that the difficult patients were the ones that had the highest survival rate.

"Who decided that?"

"Dr. Lope."

Dr. Rossi stared at her for a second. Caroline was lying on her back, looking up at him with pleading eyes. At this point, she didn't care what anybody thought of her.

"Open your mouth as wide as you can for me," he asked gently. She had to do this again? It made her feel ridiculous but she did it as best she could in her drowsy state.

"Hum...We should be able to avoid the procedure. What do you think?" Dr. Rossi turned to Dr. Clark. "Yes, looks okay to me."

"Well, it should be all right. We'll be ready for you in a few minutes, Mrs. Sauvé."

They disappeared through the swinging doors. Caroline lay on the gurney, shivering under a see-through thin blanket. She prayed for more courage. The doors swung back open. She was wheeled into a small room with painted cabinets and silver-coloured drawers. On the counter, glass containers full of long sticks reminded her of jars for spaghetti.

They slid her onto a cold metal table in the middle of the room. By this time, she looked forward to being unconscious. From past experience, she knew that it wouldn't hurt to be put to sleep. The worst part was the needle inserted into the arm but she could handle needles.

* * *

Caroline woke up in a bed with metal bars pulled up on either side. She felt like a baby in a crib. Blurred faces looked down on her. She was confused, couldn't speak. She saw a man at the foot of the bed in an immaculate white coat. Was that a worried look across his face?

Then she heard a woman's voice say from somewhere above her head: "You're healed. We healed you."

From a distance, a man's voice replied: "Now that isn't exactly true."

What did this mean? What was it about? Her eyes were heavy then closed. She fell back asleep.

* * *

It was early morning and she lay in the bed. Caroline had turned fifty. Starting a new decade of life in the hospital wasn't her first choice. She felt groggy from the pain medication but relieved that she had good news from Dr. Pine. He'd told her that they were able to repair the heart. "I am proud of you," he'd added in a loud voice. These words had made her happy but they seemed strange, more like what a family member would say than a doctor whom she didn't know.

Several birthday cards were on the window sill. One was missing, the one from Thomas. He always wrote something touching in the card like, "To my beloved," or "To my one and only love." She stared at the cards and bouquets of flowers she'd received. She had family and friends who cared. Maybe she could live without Thomas. She had gotten through this operation, hadn't she?

* * *

Mr. Bennett occupied the bed facing Caroline's. He was also Dr. Pine's patient, and was scheduled for an operation the next morning. As he settled in, Caroline had tried not to watch him but there was little other activity in the room. Mrs. Coffey lay on her pile of pillows with the sheet pulled up to her chin. Mr. Pinto and Nina were hidden behind the curtain. Caroline was sedated and could barely move because of the pain from the surgery.

Mr. Bennett, a well-preserved senior, had changed from black pants and a black turtleneck sweater to a blue hospital gown. He'd talked in a prim tone with the nurse. How come men were now admitted in the same wards as women? Caroline wondered. This had happened in the last few years. Paulina said Quebec was becoming more of a socialist country. The threadbare sheets and peeling paint reminded Caroline of hospitals she'd seen on the news reports from war zones.

Mr Bennett wanted attention. He unpacked some of his toiletries from a leather briefcase and muttered to himself, then looked around as if he needed to say something to someone. Caroline closed her eyes to pretend she was asleep. Mr. Bennett irritated her as he bustled around in his hospital gown. Couldn't he see that everyone needed quiet?

Then Mr. Bennett tried to make a call on the ward's boxy beige telephone. It looked like one of the first Touch Tone's ever made. Caroline remembered how sticky it was from all the sweaty fingers that had used it. Mr. Bennett sighed. She took pity on him as she could see he didn't understand how to dial out.

"You have to press nine first." It took an effort to project her voice and made her a bit breathless.

"I know that, dear, but it still doesn't seem to connect. I just want to call my mother, to let her know I'm here. Why can't I get through?" he asked plaintively.

Anyone who called her "dear" melted her a little so Caroline spoke more gently:

"Is it long distance? You might need to dial zero for the operator then." Mr. Bennett took advantage of her concern and explained: "My mother is ninety-nine years old and in a nursing home in Regina. She'll be a hundred next month."

Shaking his bald head, he said: "What a thing to have to tell your old mother. That her seventy-year old son is having a risky heart operation and could die."

Though there was an aisle between them, Caroline could feel Mr. Bennett's sadness. He wasn't so bad, just a little obnoxious. He cared about his mother which was decent of him. Eventually, after a few more tries and some help from the operator, Mr. Bennett reached his mother:

"Mum, it's me, James. I'm in the hospital. I'm having a big operation."

There was a pause.

"Yes, mum, I will ask Bonnie to call you to let you know how I am doing."

He hung up then slumped against the pillows.

The sun was setting and Caroline could see the lights come on in the city. All the windows were shut and the room was stuffy.

Dr. Pine, and Dr. Gordon, the resident, entered the room and marched over to Mr. Bennett's bedside. Dr. Pine politely nodded at her before turning his back. Caroline noticed for the first time how his shoulders were wide and muscular. The material of his white coat stretched tightly across them. Did he work out so he could bear the long hours of surgery?

"Good evening, Mr. Bennett," Dr. Pine said loudly as if his patient were hard of hearing. "You know you are scheduled for your operation tomorrow morning?"

Dr. Pine used his voice like a musical instrument. He could cajole, caress, or irritate with it, sometimes all three at once.

"Yes, I know." Mr. Bennett answered glumly from the shadows. The overhead light wasn't switched on.

"Don't worry, Mr. Bennett." Dr. Pine quickly added: "I will take care of you as if you were my father, or my brother."

"No, no, not like a brother," Mr. Bennett shot out. "Brothers often don't get along; they have a thing against each other...."

Dr. Pine didn't say more. He seemed to have touched a sore spot, an open wound. Did Mr. Bennett have a brother he didn't get along with? Mumbling something, Dr. Pine turned on his heel and left the room, followed by Dr. Gordon.

* * *

Caroline felt restless in her hospital bed so she pushed the electric button to make the head go up, then go down, then up again, trying to find a comfortable position. She was like a naughty child. The whirring sound probably bothered the other patients but it seemed to calm her. She finally stopped playing with the electric button and lay still. Her throat felt raw. She was woozy from the effect of the pills that Joelle, the evening nurse, had given her.

She'd rushed in, handed her the pills and a paper cup with water, then left. She seemed to have forgotten about Mr. Bennett who sat in the dark in the armchair. His bald head lolled down, his eyes were half-open, and what was also open, Caroline noticed, was his robe. She could see a glimmer of flesh down below. Could she be imagining this? She stared despite herself. Was he exposing himself to her and just pretending to be asleep? Mr. Bennett had entered the ward looking like an elegant old man. What had happened to him in the hospital?

Caroline's heart beat faster. Her arms, neck and belly felt terribly itchy. She wanted to scratch but that didn't help. She pushed the call button for Joelle. A few minutes passed before the nurse appeared and came to her bedside. Caroline whispered:

"Look, Mr. Bennett needs a blanket."

She was sure Joelle would nod and immediately go to him. The situation seemed urgent as if he had a bleeding arm. Joelle glanced in Mr. Bennett's direction and pretended nothing was amiss. Caroline spoke to her a bit more loudly this time:

"Mr. Bennett's robe is wide open. Can't you do something?"

Joelle began to giggle. She rushed out of the room and didn't return.

* * *

On her way back from the washroom, Caroline stopped to chat with Nina who sat on the metal chair by her husband's bed. Caroline didn't like to have to pull the IV pole with her. Her new bathrobe rested precariously on her shoulders as the IV tube prevented her from slipping her arm into the sleeve. She didn't even like the bathrobe which she had purchased to wear in the hospital.

At the apartment, lonely for Thomas, Caroline had flicked through the pages of the fashion catalogue to distract herself. She didn't have the energy to shop at the mall, so she'd ordered the blue cotton robe with tiny white and yellow flowers. She didn't like how the collar with wide lapels made her look frumpy like a *femme de ménage*. But why worry about what she looked like in the hospital?

Dr. Pine had come in the ward while Caroline was in the washroom. She heard him try to explain something to Mr. Bennett who kept repeating "What? What?" in his dozy state. She stopped to talk to Nina on her way back to her bed. Nina said her husband liked to have a cup of tea first thing in the morning. As Dr. Pine passed by them on his way out, he commented in his loud voice:

"Mrs. Sauvé, you can wash your hair in a day or two."

Caroline was mortified. He said it so everyone could hear. Now the attention was on the pile of sweaty, smelly hair that hadn't been washed since the operation four days ago. She struggled to find a pithy answer:

"I...would...prefer....to go to....the beauty salon...." was all Caroline could stammer out.

Dr. Pine kept smiling as if he enjoyed her discomfort. He came closer and touched her arm. He looked deep into her eyes. Probably due to the medication, Caroline imagined she saw rays of amber light shoot out of his eyes into hers as if his warmth could take shape and form.

He exited the ward. The air suddenly felt cool so Caroline, shivering, returned to her bed. She laid her dirty head on the pillows. Dr. Pine had made her feel self-conscious.

As Caroline pushed the electric button to adjust the bed, she asked herself who the doctor thought he was to tease her like that. She was beginning to believe he was attracted to her. But how could he be, the way she looked? And he was younger, no doubt married.

The day before, after the examination, Dr. Pine had done something unexpected. As he stood at the end of her bed, he'd leaned forward to grab her toes under the blanket and gave a good squeeze. This gesture seemed a little too intimate, more like something a lover, or husband, would do. Then he'd winked at her and left.

Now Dr. Pine had poked her in a vulnerable place, made her aware of her hair glued to her head by sweat, fear, and pain, the dark roots showing. Everyone could see she wasn't a natural blonde, not like Thomas whose light blond hair she'd loved. As he grew sicker, and housebound, Thomas's hair had darkened and lost its glow. He was still beautiful but she'd felt sad that he couldn't go out and walk in the sunshine as he liked to do.

"Do you want me to make you a cup of tea tomorrow morning?" Nina, who had come to her bedside, asked. "I can use this one on your table."

"Sure. That is so nice of you."

Nina took the brown plastic cup away to wash it. Caroline would have tea before the breakfast trays arrived, since Nina was allowed to boil water in the nurses' staff room. She forgot about Dr. Pine, her dirty hair, and everything else. Life was hard but there were good people about.

* * *

Mr. Bennett was the patient who could cause a commotion. He was calling out for the commode while pressing the button for the nurse.

"I need the commode," he kept repeating in a slurred manner since he was still on morphine. Caroline envied him because she had refused the two small pills that the nurse had wanted her to take. She didn't like laxatives and normally didn't need them so she hoped that somehow nature would intervene soon. She had seen Mr. Bennett swallow his pills hungrily and now he was having a reaction.

Joelle came rushing into the room.

"Bring the commode," Mr. Bennett shouted.

"Yes, Mr. Bennett. The orderly will bring it." Joelle wouldn't do it. Precious time was being lost for Mr. Bennett who was obviously in pain.

"Hurry," he said, falling back against his pillows.

The orderly wasn't long to come with a wooden chair that looked like an antique. He closed the curtain around the bed. "Ow! Ow!" Mr. Bennett complained. Soon everyone could hear embarrassing sounds and then a terrible odour invaded the ward. Caroline looked out the window to distract herself. Grey clouds hovered over the city like raw wool and the two flags fluttered in the wind. She wished her window could be opened but she didn't have the strength to do it herself.

The orderly had helped Mr. Bennett back into his bed, flung the curtain open, and emptied the commode in the toilet with several flushes. The odour was dissipating but Caroline still felt nauseated like the time she had walked into Thomas's hospital room and almost choked. He'd been moved into a semi-private which might have been a good thing except that the room was really a single, fitted with two beds facing each other. There was hardly space to stand and no chair to sit on. The window was on the side of the other bed and in that bed was a young man who looked comatose.

Mr. Neufeld, Thomas's father, was standing by the doorway and had a crazed look in his eyes when Caroline arrived. Thomas was paler than she'd seen him the day before.

"What is going on here?" she asked Mr. Neufeld. Caroline tried to keep her voice down but she was furious about the foul smell. Obviously Thomas's neighbour hadn't been cleaned.

"It's been like this for several hours," Mr. Neufeld answered.

"Didn't you call the orderly?" she asked him a bit harshly.

"Yes," Mr. Neufeld said with a sheepish look, "but they don't do anything."

Caroline wondered how Mr. Neufeld could have let this go for so long. She didn't blame the poor patient who had to bear being in what amounted to a dirty diaper. He couldn't speak for himself. She went to Thomas and touched his thin hand. He didn't say a word but his sunken eyes spoke of his distress. She could never get used to seeing him with an oxygen mask but this kept him alive.

"Let me take care of this," she said. Her rage propelled her into the hall in search of Thomas's nurse, whoever she was. Why couldn't Mr. Neufeld be more assertive? Perhaps she wasn't being fair to a man who was over seventy and recently widowed. But why couldn't he have taken care of this situation better?

At the nursing station, Caroline didn't recognize any of the nurses so she spoke to the first one that looked her way:

"Could you please send an orderly to room 925? The patient needs cleaning and it's been several hours apparently."

"Yes, we will send someone in a minute."

Caroline could have spit, wanted to cry out, but she controlled herself. As she walked down the hall back to Thomas's bedside, she sensed the bitterness she felt was due to losing hope for better days.

* * *

The ward was bright and quiet. The lunch trays had been distributed by a glum-faced orderly to Mrs. Coffey, Mr. Bennett, Gino, hidden behind the curtain, and Caroline. She sat in the blue armchair, her knees squished under the rollaway table. The food on the pink tray looked appetizing. A bright yellow omelette, still warm, smelling of fresh eggs, took up most of the plate, with a serving of buttered green beans. She felt the first twinge of hunger since before the operation and picked up the fork to take some omelette.

Just as she was about to eat her first bite, Dr. Pine arrived. He must have sensed her irritation as he said with a serious air: "I'm sorry." Caroline put her fork down. He took a corner of the table and rolled her lunch away from her. Then, before she could take another breath, Dr. Pine lunged towards her as if he were going to kiss her. He placed his stethoscope to her chest, examined the incisions under the robe and then straightened up. "You can go home tomorrow, Mrs. Sauvé."

These words didn't make her happy as he probably thought they would. Home for her meant an empty apartment, except for the cat. How would she be able to get well without Thomas beside her? "Are you sure I'm ready?" she asked, her voice shaking.

Dr. Pine probably wasn't used to patients questioning him about going home but he didn't show it. "Yes, Mrs. Sauvé." Caroline didn't want to tell him why she felt nervous to leave the hospital so she remained silent.

"*Bon appétit,*" Dr. Pine said with a smile as he rolled the table back over her knees. Caroline looked down at the plate on the tray. The warm omelette had congealed into the usual cold lump of hospital food.

Dr. Pine crossed the aisle to Mr. Bennett's bedside. He spoke loudly to him as if he feared Mr. Bennett would pass away if he didn't. What a strange doctor he was. He confused her. He was attractive but she couldn't read him at all. He cared about his patients but he was there almost too much and it was unnerving.

Caroline ate some of the cold omelette. She had to eat if she wanted to be well.

* * *

Just as Dr. Pine left the ward, Tara appeared in the doorway. She was unexpected and Caroline was glad to see her. Tara gave her a quick kiss on the cheek then handed her a magazine.

"Oh, you know how I like magazines!" Caroline exclaimed. "Thank you so much."

"I thought it would be more enjoyable than a book right now."

"Yes, my concentration isn't great with the medication, that's true." Caroline agreed. "I'm really glad you're here." She could tell Tara, whose red hair added a bright touch in the ward, the news that she was going home.

The orderly came to take away her lunch tray. Caroline lay down on her bed. Tara fluffed the pillows for her then sat in the blue armchair.

"I just got the news that I can go home tomorrow." Caroline confided. She felt queasy again at the thought.

"That's great. You don't seem happy though. Is everything okay? Do you have anyone to drive you home?"

"Paulina said she would whenever it was time, but I haven't told her yet. It's just that I feel nervous to be home without Thomas there."

"I can come by if you need anything. I'm just a few streets away remember?"

Caroline felt touched by the offer but she knew how many responsibilities Tara had. Her husband Donald was recovering from an operation for a benign brain tumour. She also had a teenage son to cook for, and her full-time job. Caroline didn't want be a burden to any of her friends and family.

"That is so nice of you but I think I'll be fine."

Tara didn't insist then shared her good news. The family had just adopted a puppy from the S.P.C.A. They had been looking to adopt one for awhile and now had found the dog that suited them.

"It'll be good for Donald to have the company during the day."

"Oh, I'm so pleased. I can't wait to see it. What kind is it?"

"It's a black Labrador and very sweet-tempered."

Caroline learned more about the new furry addition to the family. Too soon it was time for Tara to return to the office. She kissed Caroline goodbye and left.

To dissipate her fear of leaving the hospital, Caroline flipped through the home decor magazine she had received as a gift. How she enjoyed magazines since her childhood when she read the pile on her parents' coffee table. Paulina had teased her about being such a bookworm. Her sister had preferred to go roller skating or watch television together. It was with Thomas that she'd shared her love of reading. They'd spent blissful hours browsing bookstores and discussing the classics and literary bestsellers. And they'd read and discussed their intimate journals to better understand each other.

Caroline wanted to go home when she remembered all the articles she had started and could publish. She couldn't wait now to be strong enough to sit at her computer again.

* * *

Paulina entered the ward pushing a wheelchair. Caroline could tell her sister was tense. She'd sacrificed a day of work to drive her home and resented it.

"Are you ready to go?" Paulina asked. It sounded like an order. She looked at the flower baskets on the window sill: "Are you taking all those?"

"No," Caroline answered. "I want to leave them for the nurses and staff. They've been really good to me." She liked how the nurse Sue had made her toast with jam in the evenings, and Laura had sat on her bed, held her hand, and comforted her when she felt panicky.

"Yes, that's a good idea." Paulina agreed. "Look, I left my car in a fifteen minute parking zone. Let's please hurry so I don't get a ticket."

Caroline was shaken by her sister's abrupt manner. Didn't she realize that she was weak and in pain and couldn't rush about? Caroline stood up as best she could then fell into the wheelchair, her head spinning from the effort. Paulina took her small luggage and dropped it on her lap.

The sun brightened the room which was empty except for Mrs. Coffey. Mr. Pinto had been discharged the day before and Mr. Bennett was taking a shower down the hall. Paulina pushed Caroline in the wheelchair towards the door.

"Take care, Mrs. Coffey. Say goodbye to Pat for me!" Caroline said. Mrs. Coffey nodded sadly. Her doctor had told her that she couldn't leave the hospital for another week.

Paulina stopped the wheelchair at the nurses' station. Carmella remarked that Caroline looked pretty, all dressed up. It had taken time for her to slip on the skirt, stretch her arms into the t-shirt, but she had done it on her own. Her hair was still the smelly mess that Dr. Pine had teased her about. The first thing she would do at home was wash her hair. That would feel good.

Other staff said goodbye and wished her a full recovery. Caroline thanked them. She felt reluctant to go home.

"Can you stay overnight?" She asked Paulina in the elevator.

"Oh, no, I can't, sorry. I have too much to do."

Caroline felt depressed. She really appreciated Paulina's help but she missed Thomas's calming presence.

* * *

"I'm taking Décarie then the Champlain Bridge," Paulina snapped.

"I just thought it would be quicker by the Victoria Bridge, that's all....." Caroline mumbled. She knew not to insist. In fact, she didn't have the strength to say more. She stared at the road and hoped there wouldn't be any traffic snarls ahead. She preferred the Victoria Bridge over the Champlain which had lanes closed due to constant repairs.

Caroline knew people who, like her sister, chose to face bumper to bumper traffic rather than use the Victoria, a century old iron bridge. Car tires made a rattling noise and the river was visible through the iron grids but the narrow lanes were rarely blocked. Caroline would never forget the time when she'd been in her mother's car, as a child, and a tire had blown in the middle of the bridge. When her mother had stepped out to take a look, her high heels had gotten caught in the grids. She'd had to remove her feet from the shoes then dislodge the heels. It had been a hair-raising moment though they laughed about it sometimes.

Caroline felt more like crying now as Paulina drove in silence on the expressway toward the Champlain Bridge and her home.

* * *

Once inside the apartment, Caroline relaxed on the sofa with Mel curled up beside her. She scratched the top of his head and behind his ears. How soft his orange fur felt to her touch. How much she had missed him. He purred loudly to let her know he was happy she was back. The cat always helped ease her anxiety.

Paulina finished cleaning the litter box which was kept in the hall closet. She was in a better mood now that she had gotten Caroline home safely.

"I made some chicken casserole. It's in the car. I'll bring it in after I get you some bread and milk from the grocery store. I'll warm it up and we can have some lunch."

"Sure, that is so nice of you to do all this for me," Caroline said. She felt grateful to her sister for her help.

Paulina didn't have an easy life due to her strained marriage, the care of her two daughters, and constant fatigue from her full-time job at the clinic.

She left for the grocery store. Caroline was now alone in the apartment. She dreaded being forced to spend the night by herself. Darkness was coming: she had medication for her physical pain, and for her soul, she had prayer.

CONFIDENTIAL

Ten days after the operation, Caroline sat across from Dr. Pine in his office at Mountainside Hospital. He'd listened to her heart with the stethoscope then checked the incisions. "Everything is good," Dr. Pine assured her. The sky, framed by the window, was blue and cloudless behind him.

"I do have pain." Caroline said. She breathed in and felt a tug around her heart. This worried her.

"Yes, it can be a slow recovery, no doubt. Still you must feel better today than you did yesterday? A little less pain perhaps?"

Caroline was surprised. This was the type of observation Thomas would have made.

"Yes," she admitted. "It hurts a bit less today."

"Well, you will continue to improve, Mrs. Sauvé."

She had more to say but could she trust this man? She liked his clean shaven face, the loose strand of light brown hair on his forehead, how he exuded care and didn't rush her.

"Dr. Pine, I feel depressed. I mean I know a heart operation is difficult to go through but it's also because my husband died only two years ago. He died in this hospital."

"I am sorry to hear that. I remember you said something about this before."

He was calm and respectful. She'd feared he wouldn't be interested or would be uncomfortable with her openness.

"Yes, being alone is really hard. I miss my husband very much." Should she have told him this? He was a surgeon, not a psychiatrist.

"Mrs. Sauvé, again I am sorry to hear that." Dr. Pine took a deep breath. She sensed that he was hesitating to probe further.

"What happened to your husband?"

"He died of lung cancer." She could see Thomas in the intensive care unit, body skeletal and face hidden by tubes.

"Your husband must have been very young?"

"Forty-eight years old," she replied quietly.

"Yes, that is young." Dr. Pine stood up. She tried to get up from the chair but fell back, dizzy. "Are you all right?" Dr. Pine immediately looked concerned. "Yes, thank you." She didn't want to alarm him.

"I would like you to make an appointment in a month with Nancy. Can you do that?"

"Yes," Caroline replied.

Now that Dr. Pine had listened to her with sympathy, she wanted to know more about him. How old was he? Was he married? She didn't notice family photos on his desk, only paperwork and on the beige walls, framed diplomas.

Dr. Pine accompanied her to Nancy's desk. Caroline was glad he walked close beside her as her legs were wobbly. "I will see you in a month?" Dr. Pine said, smiling. She nodded and smiled back. He had passed the test.

* * *

Joanie had offered to drive her to the hospital for her next follow-up appointment. They sat together in the waiting room which was full. Caroline wondered if she should tell her friend that she had gifts for Dr. Pine. She decided not to since her friend might influence her against giving the gifts. Instead, Caroline asked:

"Do I have too much blusher on? I probably do. I'm so pale."

"No, you look fine."

Caroline was happy with that remark. Since Thomas had died, she rarely felt that she looked "fine."

"Dr. Pine is calling your name." Joanie alerted her.

Caroline gathered her things and went to him.

"I am happy to see you." Dr. Pine said as he walked down the hall beside her, holding her chart. Just the words Caroline had hoped to hear.

"You're healing well," Dr. Pine assured her. She sat at the edge of the examination table. While he washed his hands in the tiny sink, he seemed to her different than the other doctors. She liked how he engaged himself, showed emotion.

She could see he didn't wear a wedding ring. Perhaps surgeons weren't allowed to wear rings. She didn't wear hers, the diamond ring Thomas had slid onto her finger at the ceremony in the chapel. It didn't seem right to keep it on after his death which was a kind of separation, wasn't it? Her diamond ring now rested beside his gold band in the black velvet jeweller's box. She had wanted Thomas to keep his ring on but the funeral home director intimated it could be stolen so she agreed to take it back. How could anyone be so greedy as to steal a ring from a dead man's finger?

Dr. Pine returned to his desk. As she buttoned her blouse over the new lace camisole, Caroline remembered the game her father played when she was a child. She hadn't liked the game which began when he boasted to her mother how the secretaries at the office flirted with him.

"Yes, I am sure the secretaries flirt!" Her mother remarked. She was pretty with dark shoulder-length curly hair.

"I just show them the wedding ring." Her father held up his hand. "They all run away from me when they see it."

As she disappeared in another room, her mother would say: "I don't even want to look at you right now." Her father would burst out laughing.

One day, her mother had come into Caroline's bedroom to tell her that her father had thrown his wedding ring into the river after another argument. The family house was near the Seaway and, in the summer, from the open window, Caroline could hear the ship horns blow, the sound mournful to her ears. She still felt sad when she thought of what her father had done, how his gold wedding ring lay buried at the bottom of the river.

Dr. Pine checked something on the computer. She sat down and he turned to her as if in slow motion. She sensed his fatigue. She wanted to make him feel better as he had done for her.

"You have been such a good doctor," Caroline gushed. "You have helped me so much in my recovery. Here are some gifts for you."

Dr. Pine jumped out of his chair and came around the desk to her side. She gave him the blue box first. "You shouldn't have, Mrs. Sauvé," he exclaimed though she could tell he was pleased. He reacted as if he hadn't received any gifts for a long time. He opened the blue box and felt through the tissue paper till he found the crystal paperweight. He lifted it up high to examine it just as a beam of sunlight came through the window and hit it. Caroline felt as if she were in a movie scene.

"Do you like it?"

"Yes, it's beautiful. I will keep it on my desk."

This was what Caroline had hoped he would say.

"I have another gift for you."

She handed him a book of poetry by Robert Frost, a favourite of hers. She had inscribed it: "To Dr. Pine, thank you for the best of care, Caroline Sauvé." When he read these words, she saw his eyes tear up.

"You shouldn't have, Mrs. Sauvé. You know I get paid to do this work."

"I'm just happy you like the gifts, Dr. Pine." Caroline said simply. She gathered her coat from the chair and stood up. Dr. Pine came closer. She moved away. He then offered her his hand and she shook it.

"Dr. Pine, would you be willing to be interviewed for an article I want to write on medicine?" Caroline boldly asked him. This was an idea she had mulled over recently. "Perhaps you could help me?"

Dr. Pine hesitated. "Well....aren't there other doctors who might know more?"

"No. I would like to interview you." His humble reaction touched Caroline.

"Okay, please contact my secretary when you want to see me and I will get back to you."

Caroline left Dr. Pine's office, elated. In the waiting room, Joanie fidgeted in her seat with an impatient look. Caroline couldn't wait to tell her about the good health report. She decided to keep the gift giving and the interview date to herself. It seemed too good to be true.

* * *

"I hope I'll marry again," Caroline said after a sip of hot tea then joked, "Maybe to Dr. Pine..."

"It's better to live alone." Joanie replied, ignoring her reference to the doctor.

They were at the food court in the mall, at a table for two. It was a weekday afternoon and there weren't many people. Joanie had asked if she could help her find an outfit for a wedding she was invited to. Caroline agreed since she felt stronger and wanted to help Joanie who had done so much for her.

"I really don't like living on my own." Caroline added.

"No, it's better to be alone." Why did her married friends say that? Caroline knew that Joanie wasn't happily married. She said most men were "stupid." Adam didn't talk to her, affectionate hugs were in the past, she confided. But didn't she have a husband to share worries with, and didn't she have him near her (well, in the next room) at night? Adam wasn't her best friend like Thomas had been hers. Why had he been taken from her? She sipped more tea which tasted bitter without sugar. Joanie's husband, tall and reserved, could be generous, paying for cruises in the tropics in the winter.

"Are you ready to shop? If you get tired let me know. I can drive you home."

"No, no. I'm fine. It's good to be out. And you know me, I like being in the mall."

"Okay, let's go then."

They emptied their trays at the recycling bin then made their way to the boutiques. After going in and out of several, Joanie at last found an outfit that she liked. It was a two-piece suit, pink with black trim. She held the jacket and matching skirt, still on the hanger, against herself.

"What do you think?"

"Oh, that is beautiful. The pink colour is nice. And it looks perfect for a wedding."

"Great. I'll try it on."

There was a chair by the dressing room. Caroline sat down, her legs trembling. Soon, Joanie re-appeared and modeled the outfit in the full-length mirror. It hugged her slim body and the light pink colour softened her thin face framed by auburn bangs.

"That is a lovely outfit." Caroline said.

Joanie agreed: "I'll have to get a new pair of high heels to go with it but I do like it." What made the pink jacket elegant was the black ribbon trims at the wrists and collar and the black round buttons. This reminded Caroline of something.

"Well, it's a lot more than I wanted to pay, but hey," Joanie said with a grin, "I'll just put it on Adam's credit card. He doesn't mind." She disappeared into the dressing room.

A memory flashed through Caroline's mind: Jackie Kennedy on the day of the assassination of President Kennedy. She'd worn a pink outfit with black trim. Jackie had smiled and waved beside her husband in the limousine. Later she stood before the cameras, the outfit stained with his blood.

With her parents' permission, Caroline had cut photos of Jackie from the Special Edition of *Life* Magazine. She'd glued them into a scrapbook along with newspaper articles about the tragedy and wrote down her thoughts. As they watched the live television coverage, she cried with her mother and Paulina as the funeral cortege passed by. All the world's eyes were on Jackie, the widow, her face of pure sorrow protected by a black veil.

As she waited for Joanie, Caroline reflected on how as a girl, her dream had been to marry, never imagining she could become a widow.

"Okay, I'm ready," Joanie said as she rushed out of the dressing room, holding the pink outfit. "I can drive you home after I pay for this. You look a bit tired."

Caroline slowly got up. She pushed the memory of the bloody pink outfit out of her mind.

* * *

Caroline stepped out of the elevator onto the tenth floor of Mountainside Hospital where Dr. Pine's office was. The morning had started well when she turned on the radio and a song mentioned "heaven." She felt nearer heaven now as she walked down the hall past the empty waiting room to check in with Nancy, the secretary.

Caroline was so happy that Dr. Pine had agreed to the interview. She wanted to write about medicine and learn more about his research foundation. And what would she learn about him? Would she like him more, or less, after this interview?

"Dr. Pine just called and said he will be here shortly," Nancy assured her. "You can sit in the waiting room, dear." She had the look of a Hollywood star of the fifties with her wavy silver hair, round blue eyes and high cheekbones. She looked surprised to see Caroline during the off-hours, but she was discreet and didn't say anymore.

Was it only a few weeks ago that Joanie had pushed her in a wheelchair through the hospital? Now Caroline walked without being short of breath to the waiting room. Why though had she had so many cups of tea before leaving home? Should she take a chance that Dr. Pine would be late and go to the washroom? She couldn't sit through the interview like this.

She entered the washroom close by and hurried. She took a minute to reapply lipstick which was the same shade of red as her brand new sweater. After buying the sweater, she thought she might have made a mistake and called her mother in Florida for advice.

"Maybe red is the wrong colour, mom. He might not like it. He's a surgeon so red might remind him of blood."

"Oh, don't give it a second thought." Her mother brushed her frivolous concern aside. "Doctors see blood every day. I'm sure he won't make any negative connection."

Caroline hoped Dr. Pine would like the new sweater. She'd learned in a fashion magazine that men found red attractive on women.

Just as she stepped out of the washroom, Dr. Pine rushed by. He wore a long dark coat and held a pair of black gloves in one hand. She followed him. He must have sensed her presence behind him, as he turned on his boot heel and looked at her. She smiled, waving towards the washroom so he knew that was where she'd been. He nodded hello.

"I will be with you in a moment. Have a seat in the waiting room."

Caroline sat down and held her coat in her arms. At least she had experience interviewing people. She had never interviewed a surgeon before. On the phone, Dr. Pine had teased her after he agreed to the meeting.

"Your questions aren't too difficult I hope?"

She laughed. He continued teasing her:

"You aren't bringing a tape recorder, are you?"

Caroline exclaimed: "Oh, no!" though she had thought of bringing her tape recorder. Then she'd decided against it since it was an outdated model and wouldn't look professional. She preferred to take hand-written notes anyway.

Dr. Pine returned for her. He had slipped into his white lab coat. She liked to think of it as his "angel coat" since, during her research, she had learned that in Germany, it was referred to as an e*ngel hemden* or "angel shirt."

"Come with me." He walked beside her to his office. She sat down in one of the chairs and busied herself taking her notepad and pen out her bag. Dr. Pine got comfortable behind his desk. The computer was on. He held up his cell phone:

"I'm sorry. We might be disturbed by calls which I have to take...."

."That's okay," she answered in her sweetest tone. She wanted to show Dr. Pine that she appreciated any time he could give her.

As if on cue, the cell phone rang.

"Yes, yes, Dr. Matou," Dr. Pine said, swivelling his chair so she saw him in profile. "What can I do for you? Sure, I can do that. Mr. Jory, yes, the man has a small tumour on his buttock. We don't quite know what to do for him. Yes, on his right buttock..."

Each time he spoke the word "buttock," Caroline wanted to giggle. Dr Pine talked loud as he liked to do and threw her a glance from time to time. Caroline kept a straight face until she couldn't anymore then she smiled tightly.

"The poor man," Dr. Pine kept repeating. Caroline felt his compassion. When he said the name of Dr. Matou, all she could think of was Dr. Tomcat as that was what *matou* meant in French. He probably mispronounced the name. She was glad when Dr. Pine turned the cell phone off and gave her his attention:

"So sorry, Mrs. Sauvé!"

She liked how he apologized often for a doctor.

"Not a problem."

"Are you ready with your questions, Mrs. Sauvé?"

She nodded then looked down at her list. Should she start with the first question, or the second? It was fun to be with Dr. Pine. Things moved around him, unblocked, healed. She decided to go for the first. It was perhaps a little forward, but then so was being there with him:

"How old are you, Dr. Pine?"

He rolled his eyes.

"You know my age," Caroline bantered. "So it's your turn."

She was always amazed at how she could come out of her shell and say things like that to Dr. Pine.

He smiled: "I'm forty-two years old."

So she'd guessed right. He was a few years younger than her. She used to look young for her age though now she felt she looked older since the loss of

Thomas and the heart operation. She continued with the next question on the list:

"Where were you born?"

"Sherbrooke, Quebec."

Caroline was familiar with this hilly city in the Eastern Townships. Dr. Pine had pursued medical studies in the United States. She inquired about his research foundation. He told her his workload was overwhelming since there were not enough specialists in Quebec. He wished he had more time to give to his foundation. She continued with her questions. She asked him about his specialty and gathered quotes that would be interesting to include in the article. Dr. Pine spoke with enthusiasm. Caroline felt a bit self-conscious about her next question but she had to know:

"Dr. Pine, are you married? Do you have children?"

"No, I'm divorced. I don't have children." Then he added: "I have a girlfriend."

Caroline thought that a girlfriend didn't seem too serious.

"You won't include that in the article will you? I really don't want personal information in the article. In fact, we agreed that I would read the article before it is published, right?"

"Yes, Dr. Pine." Her firm response reassured him. Caroline understood that being a doctor, he wanted to protect his reputation. She asked her final question:

"Do you plan to stay in Quebec?"

"Well, my family is here. One reason I would move is for a better salary." Caroline felt a lot of sympathy for Dr. Pine. "Yes, well, I know about low pay, being a writer....." She had no idea how much a specialist made.

"Maybe I should work in another province or even the United States."

"Oh no, please don't move. We need you here."

Dr. Pine looked at her but didn't answer one way or the other.

"Thank you so much for your time." Caroline slipped her note pad and pen in her bag.

"I liked your questions. Do you have any more for me?" Dr. Pine asked. He had a big grin on his face which made him look much younger.

She thought that was sweet:

"No, not now. Thank you."

When she reached for her coat, she flinched. Dr. Pine came over to her: "Are you all right?"

"Yes. Just some discomfort." He gently helped her to slip into her coat.

"Please call me if you have more questions. In fact, you could email me."

"Sure, that's a good idea." Caroline felt excited. Having Dr. Pine's email address would open up an easy way to contact him, a much faster way than to leave a message with Nancy. Dr. Pine returned to his desk and scribbled on a piece of paper then gave it to her. She felt he'd given her something precious.

"Well, thank you again, Mrs. Sauvé. Good luck with the article."

"Thank you for giving me of your time," she repeated.

They stood in the hall. Dr. Pine approached her but she panicked and turned her face away. He didn't seem offended at all, just amused, his amber eyes full of light.

* * *

The waiting room was so busy that Caroline had to look hard to find an empty seat. She finally spotted one near the window. She made the appointment with Dr. Pine because she still had pain. Before their meeting for the interview a few weeks earlier, he'd told her to see him for a follow-up appointment in two months. It was not quite two months but Nancy had given her an appointment so it must be okay.

Caroline heard Dr. Pine's voice calling a name out. She didn't expect her name to be called since she was early. A white-haired man slowly got up and his wife, or companion, held his arm to steady him. Dr. Pine stood at the front with a chart in hand. He looked annoyed and as the couple shuffled towards him he said in a loud voice:

"I apologize for the wait, Mr. Lavoie. I can't help that as I am overwhelmed with patients. Not enough doctors you know." He hurried ahead of Mr. Lavoie down the hall.

People around Caroline were coughing, moving restlessly, some dozing in their seats. She decided to pass the time by looking at the magazine she had brought with her and pulled it out of her bag. Thomas had taught her to beware of the piles of magazines in waiting rooms since germs were rampant there. She had brought a *Victoria Look* magazine that had quotations of poetry and photos of romantic decor.

One late night, before the operation, she'd sat at the kitchen table with a home decorating book. She couldn't write anything original as she was too anxious, so she copied the text of the book in her journal. Just writing something down soothed her. She always had a pen and notepad in her bag so she could jot her observations or ideas. She would write in her journal what happened with Dr. Pine today when she got home.

"Mrs. Caroline Sauvé."

At last, Dr. Pine was calling her. She slipped the magazine back into her bag and stood up. His smile had no warmth; it was just a polite stretch of the lips. He gestured for her to follow him. He walked ahead of her and kept silent. Usually he walked beside her and asked her how she was.

She entered his office and sat down on one of the chairs. He sat behind his desk.

"Well, Mrs. Sauvé, tell me why you came today, please." There was an edge to his voice that made her feel shaky.

"Well, I have some pain. I am not sure why I still have pain....." Dr. Pine replied impatiently. "Mrs. Sauvé, I will take a look but I have explained to you that some patients can have pain for up to a year after the operation. This is not unusual. Please go to the examination table."

She did as she was told. He took her blood pressure, listened to her heart with the stethoscope. He lifted a corner of her blouse and glanced at the incisions then let go of the blouse.

"There is nothing wrong. As I said, you can have pain and discomfort for several months after the operation. Are you taking your medication?"

Caroline nodded. Dr. Pine returned to his desk. She sat down facing him. He took a deep breath and looked at her.

"Mrs. Sauvé, I am a very busy surgeon. Every day, I have more patients. I have given you a lot of my time and if I did that with all my patients..."

Dr. Pine jerked his right arm up and made a pulling gesture as if he were tightening a noose around his neck. "You wouldn't want me to have a burnout, would you?"

Caroline was astonished by his sudden change of manner towards her. She hadn't known he could get so angry. She kept quiet.

"You must follow the schedule of appointments. Your next one is in two months."

Dr. Pine stood up and Caroline did the same. She was anxious to leave, embarrassed by his behaviour. Dr. Pine opened the office door wide. As she walked past him, he gripped her elbow and hurried her down the hall to his secretary's office.

"See that Mrs. Sauvé has an appointment in two months, Nancy, not before." He grabbed a chart from the large pile on the desk and, after saying a curt goodbye, left to call out the name of his next patient.

Nancy wrote a date on an appointment card and gave it to Caroline. She didn't seem stressed by Dr. Pine's manner but Caroline was outraged. How dare he manhandle her like that! She had never had a doctor throw her out of his office. This was unacceptable; she didn't want to ever see him again. She tore up the appointment card when she reached the lobby and threw the bits in the first trash container she passed by.

That evening, Caroline sat at her computer and typed a letter addressed to Dr. Pine. She wanted something more official than an email. Her decision was made. She asked that her chart be transferred to another specialist. She didn't give him a reason why. He could figure it out.

When she dropped the letter in the mailbox at the corner of her street, she felt relieved, as if she had been freed from his grip.

* * *

Caroline turned on the television to watch the evening news. She sat on the sofa with Mel curled up into an orange ball, asleep at the other end. She'd filled his bowl in the kitchen with dry cat food and changed the water in his other bowl. She'd eaten a toasted tomato sandwich and now was sipping a cup of tea. Somewhere she had read that tea quenched thirst and dissipated sorrow. Well, she certainly drank many cups of tea each day but somehow she still felt sorrow.

She should have gone to the prayer group at the church at six pm but it was six thirty and she felt too exhausted to meet her friends there. She felt restless but without a desire to do anything but sit and stare at the television screen. The murmur of the newscaster was the only sound in the apartment. She kept the sound low because she didn't really want to hear the news. Outside, the light was growing dim. It would be another evening alone, another day ending without an answer to the question where did she go from here.

Caroline knew she didn't want to stay in this apartment which she'd shared with Thomas. It was expensive for her and more important she was reminded of Thomas' absence here. Soon after his death, the telephone often rang, and when she answered, no one was at the other end. At least no one spoke though she sensed someone there. These calls had finally stopped but it had spooked her. One evening, on a TV talk show, she'd heard a psychic explain that the newly departed tried to communicate with their loved ones by various means such as making the telephone ring. Had those calls been from Thomas trying to reassure her that he was near? She didn't know.

Now as she healed from the surgery, she felt strong enough to think about moving. But where could she move to? Did she want to stay in this neighbourhood? Did she want to relocate to another city? She had moved often with Thomas because of noisy neighbours or the rent increasing beyond their budget. She remembered how much energy it took to pack. Her parents now lived in Florida and she didn't want to move so far. Paulina lived in Montreal which appealed to her more. But she would miss being near Joanie and Tara. She would just have to bide her time.

Caroline had another sip of tea. She looked at the TV and thought about turning the sound up when the telephone rang. It startled her. Who could be calling at the supper hour? She wasn't expecting a call. She answered, her voice a bit shaky:

"Hello?"

"Mrs. Sauvé? It's Dr. Pine. Dr. Ken Pine. How are you? I hope I am not disturbing you at your supper?"

"No, no. It's okay." Caroline answered politely, her guard up. She couldn't believe she was hearing Dr. Pine's voice. It had been three weeks since she mailed the letter asking for her medical chart to be transferred to another specialist. She hadn't heard anything from his secretary. She hadn't expected Dr. Pine to call.

"Mrs. Sauvé, I received your letter." He paused then asked in a gentle tone. "Did I upset you in any way?"

Caroline was amazed that he was so direct. She thought he must know that his behaviour had been rude but she couldn't imagine discussing it.

"I really don't want to talk about that."

"Oh...."

There was a second of silence then Dr. Pine continued in his voluble manner:

"Are you sure you would like to see another specialist? I can ask my secretary Nancy to transfer your chart but I would really like if you came back to my clinic."

Dr. Pine had a way to make a professional request sound personal. It was the inflection of his voice, how he made it intimate. He was no longer the surgeon on his high horse, irritated because she took more of his time than she should. He now sounded like a man courting her back, or trying to anyway.

"I don't know," Caroline answered. She really didn't know if she wanted to see him again though he touched her by his effort.

"Please think about it, Mrs. Sauvé. It is important that you have a follow-up. What you have suffered is serious and you don't want to have complications. You would be very welcome in my clinic if you decide to come back."

Caroline sensed that Dr. Pine was sincere and this call was his way to make amends.

"I will think about it."

"Good. When you have decided, please let Nancy know. She will take care of your chart."

"Okay, I will."

"Have a good evening then!"

"Thank you."

Caroline hung up the phone. Her mind was alert as if Dr. Pine had given her an injection of powerful vitamins. She went over and over his invitation to see him. Would she? How could she not, when he called her on a Sunday evening, probably from his home? He wanted to see her again. This surprise phone call made her feel hopeful. Perhaps now she had her answer for the future.

A NEW PLACE

Paulina found a parking spot along Queen Mary Road. Caroline wasn't impressed by the high-rise building with plain windows and cement balconies. She had already visited a few buildings and none of them felt right. This one didn't look right either. Paulina insisted someone from the clinic where she worked, lived there and said it was a quiet building which was important to Caroline. Since her sister had been good enough to drive her here, she would give it a chance.

They climbed the front steps and entered. There was a security code to reach the superintendent.

"Oui?" A male voice issued from the intercom.

"Do you have a studio apartment available? We'd like to see one."

"Yes, yes, I have."

The man buzzed them in. Caroline immediately felt different about the building once in the foyer. Mahogany paneling and two massive brown leather chairs created a British style interior. A huge brass chandelier with electric candles hung above their heads. She loved chandeliers, any kind. She remembered how as a teen, she'd worked as a sales clerk in a downtown department store with a massive crystal chandelier reputedly from a *fin de siècle* cruise ship. This gave the store a romantic atmosphere she'd enjoyed.

Off the foyer, Caroline noticed a salon with a sofa, armchairs, a glass coffee table, and large brass pots with branches of eucalyptus.

"Do you want to sit down?" Paulina asked her.

The superintendent arrived before Caroline had time to answer.

"Bonjour! I'm Mr. Bourret."

They shook hands. He was about forty years old, with thick black hair and friendly brown eyes. "I have a studio on this floor." He danced on one foot than another. This was a good sign to have a superintendent who was lively and dressed in a clean pair of pants and shirt. Caroline nodded. "Oui, oui."

"Come with me," he said politely.

The comfortable decor reminded Caroline of being in a boutique hotel. The long corridor was painted buttercup yellow and by each mahogany wood door, there was a pretty light fixture with crystal pendants. The plush carpet cushioned each step and its leaf motif reminded Caroline of a William Morris pattern. She couldn't wait to see what the studio apartment would look like. Finally, they arrived at the end and Mr. Bourret unlocked the door:

"The person who lives here uses it for a *pied-à-terre*. He travels a lot. That's why there is little furniture."

The room did look bare but that didn't matter. Caroline liked its size and the large window. "You can see the swimming pool," Mr. Bourret said. Fresh air came in when he opened the patio door. The turquoise pool was empty but it was easy to imagine walking barefoot on the flagstones. Always concerned about noise level, Caroline asked:

"Are there a lot of pool parties?"

Suddenly that thought made her nervous and she doubted that this would be a place for her to settle in.

"Non. People are quiet here. No pool parties."

Paulina asked him: "Would you have a studio apartment on a higher floor?"

"We have one on the third floor. It's the same. Someone lives there but just gave notice."

"Being higher up might be better for security," Paulina suggested to Caroline. "The patio door looks easy to open."

"It's safe here," Mr. Bourret reassured them. "We don't have any problems with break-ins."

Caroline did like to be on a ground floor but now that she lived alone, she might do better to be on the third floor. Despite the fact that she didn't like to take elevators, she forced herself to go in. The elevator was small and creaked as it went up. The door jerked open and it seemed they were back on the same floor. The decor was identical. Caroline remarked on that.

"Oui," Mr. Bourret agreed. "People can get lost in this building because of that."

They made their way down the corridor. "I am not supposed to show this apartment yet but you are interested so I will do that for you."

Mr. Bourret knocked then rang the bell. No answer. He unlocked the door and they entered an exact replica of the main floor studio except that this one looked more like a home. The floor to ceiling curtains gave it a cozy atmosphere. Caroline noticed the single bed against the wall. She would have a single bed too. The tenant had set up an office space with a computer so Caroline could do that and write more articles.

"You have a nicer view here," Mr. Bourret said as he opened the door. They stepped out onto the large cement balcony. A tall maple tree leaned branches against it and Caroline could see the pool below and a well-tended garden area. Looking up, she could see the shiny dome of Saint-Joseph's Oratory at the top of the mountain. This view was more uplifting than the one from the apartment she had seen on Côte-des-Neiges, a view of the cemetery where Thomas was buried.

"This is a really nice place. I think you'd be happy here," Paulina remarked. "Yes, I like it." Caroline grasped her sister's arm because she felt dizzy from being high up and the excitement.

They returned inside the studio. Mr. Bourret showed them the kitchenette equipped with stove and fridge. She could even fit a bistro table with two chairs. Then they peeked into a small bathroom with no window. "We will install a new tub and a new sink," Mr. Bourret said, then added: "We will also paint the apartment and varnish the wood floors."

"Can I get back to you tomorrow?" Caroline asked, a bit out of breath. Her heart beat fast. She hoped she could cope with a move.

"Sure, sure."

She liked the apartment but wanted to think about it overnight. She noticed there was an inside window ledge where Mel could sit and watch the birds in the trees. Oh, the cat!

"Are cats allowed in this building?"

This would be the deal breaker.

"Yes, you can have one cat. No dogs here though."

"I have one cat," Caroline said.

"Then there is no problem." Mr. Bourret stated happily. That was good news. She could afford the rent. It was less than the one she'd shared with Thomas. She wouldn't have a bedroom but she hadn't been sleeping there since Thomas had passed away. She preferred the couch in the living-room. And now she would be near the hospital for any emergencies or follow-up appointments.

Just as Mr. Bourret locked the apartment door, a tall young woman with curly blond hair arrived. She had a scowl on her face. "I didn't give you permission to show my place," she said angrily. Caroline smiled at her but she shrugged her shoulders. "I'm sorry, very sorry. These ladies were interested in a studio so I showed this one too." The woman entered the apartment. "Please make an appointment next time." She shut the door in their faces.

Caroline didn't mind the tenant's coldness. At least she had seen who lived there.

"Can we take the stairs? I don't like elevators very much." She turned to her sister. "Do you mind, Paulina?" She said no. Mr. Bourret smiled at them: "I like the stairs better too. It's faster." An exit door was right near the apartment.

"I will call you tomorrow morning with my answer," she promised as they stood under the huge brass chandelier in the foyer. "Yes, that's fine." Mr. Bourret assured her.

Back on the street, Caroline turned to her sister: "I think I found my new home. Thank you so much for encouraging me to look in this building."

She hugged Paulina who hugged her back.

After a good night's sleep, Caroline called Mr. Bourret at 9 a.m. to tell him she wanted the apartment. They made arrangements for her to fill out an application.

Paulina was pleased by her decision and offered to accompany her back to the building. She sat beside her as Caroline signed the lease which was for a year. She would move in three months which gave her plenty of time to pack and buy what she needed to start her new life.

* * *

Caroline found Thomas's art work in the bedroom closet which she was emptying for her move. His drawings and paintings were in a large cardboard box. As she carefully slid them out, some on brown wrapping paper, some on watercolour paper, some on canvases, she saw again how gifted Thomas had been.

Though her eyes felt gritty from dust and cat hair, she flipped through his sketchpads. He'd drawn ordinary objects such as the coffee cup with an image of Shakespeare He'd captured it in detail with coloured pencils. He'd painted the blue and white antique bowl in the living-room. A sketch of his thin hand startled her

Caroline sat on the bedroom floor like a child, papers and canvases around her. She was amazed at the monk-like quality of Thomas's face in self-portraits. She didn't want to canonize him but there had been something of the saint in him. He reminded her of a favourite artist, Vincent Van Gogh. Dutch ancestry linked them physically but also short, tortured inner lives. Thomas possessed a similar gaunt face, reddish blond hair and red beard. He had a high forehead, high cheekbones, and deep set green eyes with an intense gaze. She noticed how the drawings recalled the early sketches of Van Gogh: spindly people, and thin leafless trees that would later bloom with powerful movement and colour.

Perhaps Thomas would have developed into a great artist if he had been given his full years. Certainly his passion for art had expressed itself even in the last months, when he was in the hospital. How could she forget entering the ward one afternoon, to see him sitting up in bed, at work in his sketchbook, as he laboured for breath. He'd sketched the basket of daisies she'd placed on the window sill, just like Van Gogh, who painted flowers in the asylum. She treasured Thomas's art work more than anything else, even his diaries. Both her mother and Paulina had chosen a painting they admired for keepsakes but Caroline had kept her favourite. It hung on the wall facing the bed. Thomas had completed it just a couple of weeks before he entered the hospital for the last time.

Caroline got up from the floor to relieve the soreness in her legs. She stood in front of the painting. It represented a beautiful young woman dancing, as if out of the pages of the Old Testament, from King David's Court. She played cymbals, her mass of black hair streaming behind her. She had on a white dress with a wide purple sash and a short-sleeved beige silk jacket. A necklace made of several strands of copper coins decorated her neck. There was mournful determination in her eyes.

She felt Thomas had left her a message through this painting - that she had to keep going despite everything. She had to listen to the music from her heart and, like the gypsy woman with cymbals, she had to play her part in life. Whenever she saw the painting, Caroline felt stronger, as if the woman emitted force and spirit to her. Had Thomas consciously known and planned to leave her this positive image or was it an unconscious otherworldly message? Thomas was with her through his art, and wasn't that vivid presence what any artist, writer, musician aspired to?

She loved the painting. She couldn't wait to place it on a wall in her new apartment in the city.

* * *

67

As Caroline continued to look through the closet for things to pack, she came across her wedding dress. She kept it beside the dark green suit Thomas had worn. She had given most of his clothes away to a local charity but had kept his complete wedding outfit, including the shirt, tie and shoes. What could she do with her wedding dress? She touched the soft rayon silk material. The dress was A line and long with ivory thread embroidery on the bodice and mother of pearl buttons down the front. The neckline was square with narrow shoulder straps. During the ceremony at the chapel, she wore an ivory lace jacket to cover her shoulders and arms, and white shoes with buttons like those of a Victorian bride.

Lately, Caroline had taken to wearing the dress at night to sleep in, and it was a bit crumpled. She knew this was odd and she didn't want to become like Dickens's Miss Havisham in *Great Expectations*, who had never taken off her wedding gown after being jilted at the altar. Traumatized, Miss Havisham became an eccentric recluse, boarding her windows, living in the dark with her wedding cake decaying where she had left it on the dining-room table. She had even stopped the clocks.

Though Caroline had not been jilted, the death of Thomas sometimes felt like abandonment. She could see how someone could become bitter, full of rage at being alone again after sharing hopes and dreams with her beloved. Now she felt she had to start over and she didn't know if she could. Should she give away her wedding dress and also Thomas's bridegroom suit?

She remembered how beautiful he'd looked as he waited for her at the altar in the chapel. The wooden pews were filled with smiling family and friends who had gathered to celebrate with them. That summer morning, both she and Thomas were physically shaky. Caroline, from heart palpitations she ascribed to the stress of the wedding, and he, from the nagging cough and fatigue of his undiagnosed cancer. Yet they had met at the altar to exchange vows for eternal love.

Thomas had proposed to her when she'd been admitted to Mountainside Hospital for tests. He had brought his chair closer to the bed and taken her hand in his. "It would be a good idea to marry," he said gently. She felt the inner door open at last to complete love. They lived together but it never felt "right" to her. Despite her early divorce, she still believed in marriage, and Thomas, also divorced, overcame his resistance to the commitment. She answered "yes" as gently as he'd asked, and felt strengthened by joy. Was it Thomas's prayers that re-awakened the faith she experienced as a Catholic child? She believed again in the presence of angels, in the divine order of things.

In the downtown chapel decorated with Tiffany stained glass windows, Reverend Carsen had blessed their union. Three years later, she was bereft and alone. She wanted to keep her wedding dress; like Miss Havisham, she needed to keep it.

* * *

Caroline called Dr. Pine's office and made an appointment with his secretary. She was anxious to see him and didn't want to wait until after the move.

The air conditioning wasn't working properly in the quiet waiting room and the warm air smelled of medication and perspiration. After checking in with Nancy, Caroline sat down a few seats from a pot-bellied man and big-boned woman. She held a brown manila envelope with her recent scan and it reminded her of the brown envelope she slipped articles in for magazine editors. She wanted to start working again as soon as she was settled into her new apartment. Would Dr. Pine still be interested in the article about medicine and his foundation? More important though was what would he see on the scan?

Caroline had made sure to look well despite her fatigue. She'd washed her hair and slipped on a white lace blouse and a flowery cotton skirt. She had her flip-flops with shiny pink buttons that people said were cute. She was nervous to meet with Dr. Pine again. Would she still feel attracted to him? The last time she saw him was when he had rudely escorted her out of his office months ago. "You will be welcome," Dr. Pine had assured her on the phone.

Caroline didn't wait long before she heard his loud voice coming from the hall. Then he appeared, accompanied by a bald man in a golf shirt and shorts. The man left with a smile. Dr. Pine also smiled as he told the couple in the waiting room that he would see them next. Then he winked at Caroline. He seemed to be on an adrenaline spurt, moving near her, then away.

"It won't be long, Mrs. Sauvé."

Dr. Pine disappeared down the hall with the couple following him. She definitely felt attracted to his sweet expression and summer tanned face, his shiny brown hair, his stocky body. She was glad to have made the appointment.

It was Nancy who soon led her to Dr. Pine's office. Where had he gone, the washroom? Caroline sat down, the scan in its envelope leaning against her bare legs. She hoped again for a good report.

She heard someone take a deep breath, then the door opened wide, and Dr. Pine burst in, chart in hand.

"I am very happy to see you," Dr. Pine said brightly. The warmth from his brown eyes was like a caress on her skin. "I am very happy to see you too, Dr. Pine." He looked surprised that she would say that. He lowered his head and looked at the floor. Had he been nervous to see her? Did she make him nervous? She didn't want to.

"I have the scan." Caroline pointed to the brown envelope.

"Yes, we can look at that later. I want to take your blood pressure first."

She didn't really want to wait but he was the doctor. He wheeled up to her on a round stool and their knees touched. She noticed that his black pants were tight against his thighs and the hems were too long and fell over his scuffed shoes. He must have grabbed the last clean pair of pants from the back of his closet. His lab coat was impeccably white and without creases as usual. Now that he was so close, Caroline saw how his eyes were rimmed with dark brown circles. He looked older than forty-two.Why did doctors have to work so hard that their own health was compromised? Caroline remembered how he'd told her the last time she'd seen him that he was near a burnout. She felt a pang of sympathy for him.

After taking her blood pressure and saying it was fine, Dr. Pine asked, in his genuine manner: "How have you been?"

"Oh, I'm living among boxes," Caroline replied with a mischievous air. "I'm moving into my new apartment soon. I'll be near the hospital."

Dr. Pine looked perplexed. He didn't seem to know what to say about that, so he posed routine clinical questions about the state of her health. Satisfied by her reassuring answers, he then asked:

"Have you finished your article on medicine?"

"No." Caroline answered, taken aback by his direct question, but then that was one of Dr. Pine's specialties. "I can't yet," she added, a bit in a huff that he would think an article could be written so quickly. "I will need to ask you a few more questions before I can complete it anyway."

"Oh...yes, well, you know I am very busy, even more than most specialists. Just ask the security guard downstairs. I am one of the last to leave the hospital at night."

She believed him but she felt disappointed that he didn't offer to help with the article.

"By the way, Mrs. Sauvé, I don't think you should send me emails. I don't have time to answer you." Her face must have shown her disbelief as he added: "No one should send emails. I receive so many."

He stood up.

"Let's look at your scan."

He slid the scan out of the envelope to clip it to the light monitor. She noticed his hand trembled. "Well, it's excellent, the heart is healing well. Come here, please."

Caroline didn't want to but she went to stand by Dr. Pine. His arm grazed hers. "Look, there is your heart." He pointed to a dark shape. Was that her heart? It looked small and oval rather than the traditional Valentine drawing.

Dr. Pine turned towards her, his eyes moist. He offered his hand and she took it. Then, on an impulse, she pulled him to her and wrapped her arm around his neck. She dropped her head against his chest as if to listen to his heart beat. Hadn't she wanted to be in his arms for a long time? Hadn't he been tempting her? She could feel him tense up so she began to let go, embarrassed, but his arm wrapped around her waist, and he held her tightly against him. She relaxed in his warmth.

Caroline let go first. They moved away in opposite directions but not too far from each other. She couldn't look directly at Dr. Pine, wondering what he was thinking, or feeling. He was pretending to study her chart which he'd held onto through the embrace.

"You have experienced many trials, Mrs. Sauvé. You are a strong woman."

She didn't know what to make of what he said, except that it was obviously a compliment. What she would have liked to hear was, "I love you too," but that wasn't what he was saying. She was confused and filled up with more emotion than she could handle.

"Thank you." Caroline couldn't think of anything brighter to say. She wanted to leave right away. However Dr. Pine wanted to finish the examination.

"Sit here, please."

He pointed to the examination table against the wall. Did he expect her to lie down? No, he said "Sit here." She quickly did as told. Taking his stethoscope, Dr. Pine listened to her heart. Surely he could tell she was flustered. How could he be so cool?

"Please make an appointment with my secretary. I want to see you in three months. You know how important the follow-up is. Let me go with you."

"No, no, Dr. Pine. Don't worry. I will."

She wasn't sure if she wanted to make an appointment. She'd have to think about it after all that had happened. All she wanted was to leave the hospital. She hurried down the hall as dignified as she could manage in her flip-flops.

Outside, the heat and smog felt like a hand pressed over her nose and mouth. Caroline caught the Côte-des-Neiges bus at the corner. Tears began to flow down her cheeks even before she made it to the single seat. She stared out the window, unable to keep up with her tears, her tissue a soggy mess. What was going on with her? Why had she acted so foolishly? She had hugged a man who had a girlfriend, who had told her he didn't want her emails. Trying to stop crying, Caroline remembered that Dr. Pine had hugged her back and not pushed her away. Didn't that mean he cared for her?

"You haven't been the same since you met that doctor," her mother had said on the phone. In fact, she hadn't been the same since Thomas had died. That was probably the heart of the matter, what had gone wrong with her.

GRIEF WORK

Edwin, a friend of Thomas, lifted boxes filled with books and journals, and placed them, one on top of the other, in the walk-in closet. The temperature in the apartment was near 30 C and his brown face was slick with perspiration. Edwin had emigrated from Jamaica with his wife and children. He invited Caroline to visit his family in Jamaica which she thought was kind of him. He seemed to want to keep an eye out for her now that Thomas was gone.

Caroline was relieved that Edwin had agreed to help her order her belongings in the new apartment. She had money to offer him for his help since Thomas had provided insurance for her. To stretch it out, she would write and publish new articles. She was back on her feet, literally.

"You've got a nice place here, Caroline." Edwin remarked, his brown eyes twinkling: "Seems you are moving up in the world."

She smiled. "Yes, I really like it."

She knew what he meant. Even though the apartment was smaller than the one she had shared with Thomas, the building was more elegant. She didn't mind trading some space for a room on the mountain.

"Would you like a glass of water?" Caroline asked Edwin.

"Sure, that would be good."

As she made her way between the boxes to the kitchenette, she heard a strange noise. It was as if someone were trying to unlock the apartment door. How could that be happening? Who would have a key to her apartment? She looked back at Edwin who heard the noise also.

"Who is there?" she asked. Was it Mr. Bourret? Caroline suddenly felt trapped. Edwin stared at the door. No one answered and the key kept jiggling in the lock. She went to the door, opened it: a tall thin young man, well over six feet, stared down at her.

"Who are you? What do you want?" she demanded. Edwin came by her side, sensing that something was wrong.

"What do you want?" he repeated. The young man mumbled something, his eyes staring at the floor.

"You don't have any business here." Edwin stated. "Please go now and don't come back."

The man turned away and slowly walked down the hall. Edwin followed him until he turned the corner and disappeared. Caroline thanked Edwin for his intervention as he came back into the apartment. She locked the door.

"Weird fellow," Edwin remarked. "He must be new here and thought this was his apartment."

"Yes, you're probably right, Edwin."

This explanation made her feel more secure. She entered the kitchen for the glass of cold water. When Edwin left an hour later, with a load of empty cardboard boxes, the apartment was more spacious. Caroline felt happy again to have moved.

* * *

It was ten p.m. Caroline had just turned the light off and was resting in bed. Mel had rolled into a ball and shone like a night light at her feet. She felt less alone having him there He reminded her of the cat in *Breakfast at Tiffany's*. The orange cat in the movie had no name but she called hers Mel, short for Melville, the name of the street where she found the abandoned kitten. Mel was now four years old and looked healthy and well fed.

Her new single bed was comfortable and made her think of the narrow bed she'd slept in as a girl. She and Paulina, only two years apart, had never had to share a bedroom. Most of her friends who had sisters had to share a room as they grew up. Now she had a room and a single bed. In fact, the double bed wouldn't have fit.

"If you ever have a boyfriend, he can take you to a hotel," Paulina had teased her.

Just as she was starting to feel drowsy from the tranquilizer she took every night, Caroline heard a noise. It was a key jiggling in the lock. She sat up, her hand instinctively protecting her heart. "Who is it?" she asked. She turned the light on by her bed. She was furious thinking it must be the tall man from earlier in the day.

"Go away right now or I will call the police," she shouted out. She heard steps going down the hall. Her new neighbours must have heard also. She had to get another lock, a deadbolt. She couldn't take this stress. She had to feel safe in her own place. Mel had jumped off the bed and hid under it. Caroline lay back down. She fell asleep, the light on through the night.

* * *

Caroline woke up at eight a.m. and turned the light off. Sunshine brightened her apartment. She recalled the experience of the night before and decided to go ahead to the locksmith. The lock on her door was flimsy. She'd noticed some neighbours had two locks. A friend who lived in New York City said that tenants there had three or even four to feel safe. She just wanted one more.

At nine a.m. Caroline walked down the side street that led to a row of storefront buildings with a locksmith shop beside a butcher that made her feel queasy. She couldn't bear to look at raw meat or think of the animals being slaughtered. A bell rang as she entered the locksmith shop, a small area with cardboard boxes on shelves and a glass counter placed at a crooked angle. A bronze cash register rested on the top. Caroline wondered how it didn't break through the glass from its weight.

A big scruffy man with a beer belly appeared from the back. He said hello in an indifferent tone. Caroline asked him about deadbolts.

"I have a few models, different price ranges."

"Well, I need a good one."

"It can cost $250."

This was more than she wanted to pay and said so.

"Well, I have one for $150 but it's not as reliable. Where do you live?"

Caroline had mentioned she'd just moved in the neighbourhood. Reluctant, she told him the street address.

"Oh, that building," the man spit out. "They let anyone in there. You'd better buy the most expensive model if you want to be safe. You wouldn't want someone to break in while you were taking a bath would you?"

This thought made her nervous. Not just the suggestive image that the man conjured of her but was it true that her building was not safe even with the security system? The tall man at her door had made his way in, and might be a tenant, or might not be. She seriously considered buying the most expensive model but she could tell the other model looked sturdy too. No, she would buy the one she could afford. It would do.

"Thanks but I will buy this model." She pointed to the one she wanted. The man abandoned his sales pitch and rang up the total on the noisy cash register.

"I need it as soon as possible." Caroline added. She didn't want to wait a few days.

"Well, my son can come by in two hours or so. It'll cost you an extra $25. How's that?"

"Yes, that's fine."

She left the store with the receipt folded in her bag. She was taking care of herself. She was living in Montreal and would have two locks on her door for protection.

* * *

Caroline could feel the mid-afternoon sun burning the top of her head as she walked up Côte-des-Neiges. It would have been a better idea to go to the hardware store early in the morning, but she didn't like to be dictated to by the thermometer. In fact, she could see the digital sign by the O'Doré Bar-B-Q restaurant flash the temperature and time: 31 C at 14:20.

The street bustled with cars, and the humid air was thick with exhaust fumes. Caroline hoped she wouldn't faint like the elderly woman with a cane whom she had seen *tomber dans les pommes* in front of the bank. An ambulance had come within minutes to take the woman to the hospital.

Even though the heat was intense, Caroline felt light-hearted as she made her way in her new neighbourhood. The trees on the mountain were a lush green, and Saint-Joseph's Oratory looked like a gigantic three-tiered wedding cake. There were twenty-four hour stores and restaurants for her to lose her loneliness in.

Tired from unpacking, she hadn't had the will power to wash her hair, now stuck to her head from the humidity. In her tight white t-shirt, her straight blue jeans, and cat's eyes sunglasses, she felt like she belonged in a James Dean movie. At the hardware store, she had flirted with the funny young clerk who made a spare set of keys for her apartment. She had the extra set in her bag. Who would she entrust the keys to? She could always give them to Paulina but she might feel it an imposition. She never knew how her sister would react anyway.

Caroline neared the O'Doré Bar-B-Q restaurant. It was the one where she'd found refuge with her mother and Paulina, after the burial ceremony for Thomas at the cemetery. Caroline saw a man step out who looked familiar but the awning kept him in shadow. The man had a look of panic on his face as if he had seen a ghost. Could it be Dr. Pine? He hurried down the street looking straight ahead as if he hadn't seen her. Maybe he hadn't. What was she going to do? Let him go by without saying anything? Then Dr. Pine looked at her, just as they were passing each other, and stopped. It was nice to see him in street clothes, beige cotton pants and a chequered brown short-sleeved shirt, the style of clothes Thomas would have worn.

Caroline lifted her sunglasses off her perspiring nose. "Hello, Dr. Pine. It's good to see you."

"Hello Mrs. Sauvé," he answered. She shook his hand which was wet with perspiration.

"You live that way?" he asked, gesturing down Côte-des-Neiges. "No, that way," Caroline responded, pointing towards the Oratory and the top of the mountain.

She remembered the embrace they'd shared in his office. What could he be feeling? She wondered again if she should remain his patient.

"Dr. Pine, I really need to talk with you."

She stared into his eyes to make him feel the urgency of her request. Maybe they could go in the restaurant to talk.

"Not now, it's not possible. They just called me for an emergency." He pointed to his pant pocket where she guessed his beeper was. So that explained why he had perspiring hands. It wasn't due to seeing her but because he had to rush to the hospital. How she admired this exhausted man, who probably hadn't had time to finish his Bar-B-Q chicken before having to help someone in distress.

Dr. Pine moved away from her towards the parking lot. "Make an appointment with my secretary."

"Okay," she replied politely. He then disappeared among the parked cars.

Caroline continued her slow dizzying climb up Côte-des-Neiges. So Dr. Pine wanted her to make an appointment to hear what she had to say. That was encouraging. But it seemed like a cold response after their embrace. When he'd said, "Not now," did that mean that he would have invited her to the restaurant if he had time? Caroline imagined them sitting at a table for two in the rustic fragrant interior. It made her feel happy. She was surprised that Dr. Pine frequented the restaurant. He seemed to be more of a gourmet but O'Doré wasn't far from the hospital and had a good reputation. Her parents had ordered the chicken and fries special when she was a child, and now the chain had expanded their menu to include healthy salads, and a choice of rice, or baked potato. She liked the fleet of bright orange cars that crisscrossed the city to deliver the Bar-B-Q chicken. She saw one go by as she neared her new building.

Caroline searched her bag for the keys and her hand fell on the spare set. Hadn't she been wondering, just before she saw Dr. Pine, who she would give them to? It seemed a crazy thought but were they meant for him? Was it coincidence to have bumped into him, or was it fate?

* * *

"I'm just going for you," Paulina announced to Caroline as they walked down the street to O' Doré Bar-B-Q. The evening was cool so Caroline wore her black wool coat over her skirt and blouse. She felt high from the apple-scented autumn air and the sweet rottenness that exuded from the red leaves that strewed the cement sidewalk.

"That's fine. I really appreciate it. Who knows," she teased her, "you might meet someone at the speed dating tonight." Caroline knew that wasn't the best thing to say since Paulina was unhappily married to Rick and the solution would not be to meet someone else.

"I don't want to," her sister replied. Under the glare of the street light, Caroline noticed how carefully Paulina had done her hair and make-up, wore a designer pair of jeans and her suede jacket. Perhaps she did want to meet someone new.

A few days before, Caroline had noticed the flyer for the speed dating event on the O'Doré bulletin board. She immediately felt intrigued. She'd heard that speed dating was fun and seen a news report on TV about it. Caroline hoped this might be the night she would meet a man who would help her forget Dr. Pine. She hadn't made the appointment with his secretary as he'd asked. What was there to discuss really? He had a girlfriend, and she was his patient.

She followed Paulina up the steps into the restaurant bar where the event was taking place. It was empty but they were half-an-hour early. They chose a table at the back. The pop music was so loud they had to shout their order to the waiter. They both wanted Perrier with lemon. Paulina wasn't a teetotaller like her but she said she wasn't in the mood for wine. They slipped their coats off and glanced at the people coming into the bar. The average age seemed to be twenty-five.

"I'm going to talk to that man there at the entrance," Paulina said. "He looks like he is the organizer of this thing. Maybe he can tell us why there isn't anyone our age here." When she returned to her seat, she said: "He was nice. He explained this event was advertised at the university so the crowd will be that age group. They want to organize an event for our age group another time. They will see how this turns out first."

"Oh, then we should leave," Caroline suggested. She had finished her Perrier and the loud music was giving her a headache.

"Okay."

The event was a let-down but at least she had tried something different, Caroline told herself, as she slipped her coat back on. She followed Paulina into the dining area. A man sat alone at a table for two, hunched over a newspaper.

Caroline tugged at Paulina's coat:

"Wait, I think Dr. Pine is here."

"What?" hers sister turned to her, eyes wide and questioning.

"Yes, I'm sure it's him. I'm going to say hello."

The moment Caroline recognized Dr. Pine, she felt the urge to go to him like some primal force. She hadn't heard from him but there he was, like a physical answer. She quickly made her way to his table.

"Hi, Dr. Pine," she said cheerfully. He didn't look up from the newspaper. Was he trying to ignore her? Hadn't he recognized her voice?

"Dr. Pine. It's Caroline." Then she remembered he never addressed her by her first name, even though she had asked him too. "It's Mrs. Sauvé."

He slowly looked up from his newspaper. No smile to break the ice cube that was his face. She was so pleased to see him that her warm smile, she was sure, could melt an iceberg. She wished he would invite her to join him at the table and call him Ken. She thought of boldly sitting in the empty chair but resisted.

"Dr. Pine," she rattled off. "I'm so glad to see you. I came with my sister." She stopped to search for Paulina who now stood by the exit. "I want you to meet her."

She left to get her sister who looked sour as if she had drunk lemon juice rather than Perrier. Caroline was so excited to be able to introduce her that she didn't care what she felt.

Dr. Pine looked good in his black pants, white shirt with blue pin stripes, and a navy blue tie. After all these months that Paulina had heard about him, she would at last meet him. And he would meet her sister.

Caroline was back at his side before he'd had time to turn a page of the newspaper.

"Dr. Pine, this is my sister. Paulina, this is Dr. Ken Pine."

Something felt wrong. Dr. Pine didn't stand up to greet her sister and Paulina said a tepid hello then told him: "I took care of Caroline when she was recovering from the operation. I'm a receptionist at a clinic." Dr. Pine didn't respond. Caroline wondered why he was so tense.

"I'm going to wait for you outside," Paulina stated abruptly then left. Caroline guessed that her sister was going to go smoke a cigarette which was not something the doctor would approve of.

Caroline wasn't ready to go. Dr. Pine seemed to have recovered from the shock of their meeting.

"Mrs. Sauvé," he began, "you need to see a specialist for a follow-up. If you don't come to my clinic, I recommend you see Dr. Corey, or Dr. Demers."

"I will think about it." Caroline responded, glad he still cared about her health. She didn't want to see another doctor, but she might have to considering how complicated it was with Dr. Pine.

"You must have a follow-up. You don't want to get ill again."

"No, I don't."

At last, he smiled at her.

The waiter arrived with Dr. Pine's order of Bar-B-Q chicken. He was having a late supper at nine p.m. He probably needed the food to build his endurance. Caroline felt depleted, ready to say goodbye. Paulina must have finished her cigarette and would be waiting for her.

"It was so nice to see you. Have a good evening."

Her earrings jingled as she walked away. Dr. Pine could make her feel feminine and youthful. He'd even said a few times: "You are so young!"

Outside, the dark air was cool. She joined Paulina who acidly stated: "Your doctor didn't seem to like what I said." Caroline defended him gently. "I think he was just shocked at meeting like that. That's all." It had been rude that he didn't stand up to shake her hand.

They walked up the street towards Caroline's building and the car parked in front.

"He seems to be in his own world, that's for sure," her sister added. And he's quite ordinary looking. I wouldn't be able to find him in a crowd."

Caroline felt deflated. How could Paulina not see how adorable he was? He might not look like a movie star but he had pleasant regular features. His light brown hair was shiny and he dressed well.

"We don't have the same taste in men and that's good." Caroline joked. "I wouldn't want you to be attracted to him and take him away from me."

Paulina shrugged her shoulders. Caroline could see her perfect profile against the dark sky. What had Dr. Pine thought of her sister? They reached the car and exchanged a goodnight kiss which was made unpleasant by the stale cigarette breath.

"Thanks for coming with me."

"We can talk tomorrow."

Paulina drove off as soon as Caroline entered her building. She felt thrilled from the incredible turn of events. She'd made an effort to meet someone to forget Dr. Pine and who did she meet? Dr. Pine. Who could explain that to her? Everything was all right. He cared about her, about her health at least. And she cared more about him each time they met.

* * *

Caroline arrived a few minutes early for her lunch date with Tara at the fast food restaurant. She decided to sit outside on a bench to wait. It was at a busy downtown intersection where cars whizzed through the yellow light and sometimes the red light.

The narrow square had newly planted trees and a statue of Dr. Norman Bethune. Caroline didn't know a lot about him except that he was a Canadian surgeon who died a hero in China. The statue wasn't impressive in her eyes. The white stone didn't give substance to the statue which looked like it belonged in a cemetery. Pigeons used the bald round head to sit on and there were droppings everywhere. She remembered how the City had tried to poison the birds but numerous petitions had stopped this effort to decimate them.

Tara arrived breathless from her quick walk. They hugged each other then entered the restaurant. It was conveniently close to Tara's office building. They each chose a soup and sandwich combo at the counter. While Tara waited for their order, Caroline slipped into an empty booth and wiped crumbs off the table with a napkin. She gazed at Tara whom she hadn't seen since her visit at the hospital. She looked statuesque with thick red hair. Tara deposited the tray with soup and sandwich before her.

"So how have you been?" Tara asked with a slight Irish accent that Caroline liked. It brought to her mind James Joyce's story "The Dead." Every time she read it, she was transported to that New Year family dinner then the cold bedroom where the main character learned more about his wife's past. Caroline also mourned her lost lover but she didn't have a Gabriel to hold and comfort her.

"How is Donald?" Caroline asked Tara, who had started to eat her barley soup.

"He's doing well but he still has to rest a lot. The dog has cheered him up though and he goes for long walks with him."

Caroline felt a twinge, no, a stab of envy. It was wrong but she couldn't help it. It didn't seem fair that she had lost Thomas but Tara still had Donald.

"I am so happy for you that Donald is doing better."

She meant every word yet there was a bitter taste in her mouth as she swallowed spoonfuls of tomato soup. Why did she have to feel so much that even her taste buds were affected?

"Thanks," Tara answered quietly. She didn't seem as happy as Caroline would have imagined.

"Donald feels frustrated not to be able to work. He gets up and tries to do things around the house but then he feels weak and has to sleep for hours."

"I know. Convalescence takes a lot of patience. He has to be careful not to overdo it."

"Yes, well, it's not easy for him being cooped up in the house."

Caroline looked at Tara across from her. Her face had an unusual pallor and looked puffed. She now had the burden of being the family breadwinner. Still she'd been spared the loss of her husband. Tara had known Thomas and liked him. This meant a lot to Caroline. When she was with someone who hadn't known Thomas, she felt even more bereft.

What could she do now but eat her soup and sandwich and be a friend to Tara? Hadn't Tara been a friend to her when she comforted her after Thomas's death and visited her in the hospital after the operation? She wanted to be a support to Tara who now faced having a fragile, physically weak husband, something she knew about.

Tara looked at her watch.

"I have to get back to the office. I can't be late as I have a meeting."

"Okay," Caroline said, forcing a smile. Time was not flexible around Tara. She had appointments, clients, responsibilities. Caroline had her own work to do though she had more free time. She wished she could be with Tara longer but that wasn't possible.

Outside, in the sunshine, they exchanged a kiss and promised to meet again soon. Caroline walked to the bus stop, and as she passed the statue of Dr. Bethune, she wondered if Dr. Pine knew something more about him. She could ask him if they ever spoke again.

* * *

Caroline sat at a table with Paulina at O' Doré Bar-B-Q. They were on a wooden platform like a stage. Caroline could easily see the electric fireplace in the middle of the restaurant. She liked the glow of the fake logs which gave the illusion of red flames. It was dark and icy outside, and the people waiting in the line-up to be seated, looked happy to be inside.

Paulina had called earlier in the day: "I'm inviting you to eat out tonight." It sounded more a command than an invitation.

"That is so nice of you, sure."

"It's bitterly cold so I will pick you up, okay?"

Caroline agreed. She had been working too many hours. It was the beginning of the New Year and minus 20 C. They were crazy to venture out but she sensed Paulina was stressed with Rick away on a business trip. Marie and Jennie, her nieces, were probably curled up on their beds with their school work and talking to friends on their cell phones.

Caroline lifted her eyes from the menu as the young waiter arrived to jot down their orders. They both chose the chicken pot pie special and coleslaw on the side. When he'd left, Paulina stated: "You have to eat all your coleslaw. I just read in a health magazine that cabbage is excellent for the circulation."

"Yes, well, I will eat as much as I can but it's hard to digest." Caroline answered. It was a bit irritating to be told what she should eat. She didn't like to think of food as some medical substance.

"I like to cook that angel hair cabbage that comes in a plastic package," Paulina said. "I just throw it in a pan with some sliced onions and a bit of soy sauce and it's delicious."

"Well, you have a stronger digestive system than I do, you always have."

Paulina didn't say anything more and took a sip from her glass of water. The waiter arrived with the pot pies.

"Wow, that's a huge portion." Caroline remarked.

"Well, you have to eat it all." Paulina insisted.

Caroline laughed. "I'll try for half."

She'd often been told she ate "like a bird" since she preferred to snack throughout the day.

As they ate their pot pies, Caroline remembered how, the last time she'd been in the restaurant with Paulina, she'd bumped into Dr. Pine. Wouldn't that be an amazing coincidence if he came in the restaurant now? Only a week ago, she'd sent him a card to wish him Happy New Year and included a small gift that fit in the envelope, a pewter coin with the word *"harmony"* engraved on it. She'd chosen that one from a big bowl with coins for *"wisdom,"* *"joy,"* *"peace,"* among others.

She thought he would like the word since he'd told her he listened to music to relax. And harmony was also the wish she had for their relationship. He must have received the letter but she hadn't heard from him by phone, or even email.

"This sauce is very rich," Paulina admitted, putting down her fork. "I'm sure they used cream not milk. I don't think I can eat all this."

"Yes it is very rich. I guess you won't expect me to finish it either then?" Caroline teased then added, "Listen, I drank a lot tea. I have to use the washroom."

"Go. I'll check the dessert menu. We could share something."

"Well, maybe," Caroline said though she knew she couldn't eat another bite.

She got up from the table making sure she had her bag so she could put on lipstick. She made her way down the platform steps, and when she approached the stairs to the lower level where the washrooms were, she noticed a man studying a flyer near the cash register. He stood right under a ceiling spotlight and turned towards her.

It was Dr. Pine smiling and looking like an angel in the glow of the spotlight. Caroline thought a harp should be playing in the background rather than the pop music. She sensed he'd been waiting for her and only pretended to read the restaurant flyer.

"Happy New Year, Mrs. Sauvé. How are you?"

"Well, you seem to be here all the time," Caroline blurted out. She regretted her words. Dr. Pine took a step back.

"I guess you like the food here," Caroline hastily added. "It's really good." Then she rubbed her stomach like a child would, to make her point.

"I want to thank you for the card and the coin. I really like the coin," Dr. Pine said.

"Oh, I'm glad you received it." She was so happy to see him, she felt overwhelmed. "Excuse me. I was going to the washroom."

"Okay. I wish you a Happy New Year."

Caroline nodded then hurried down the stairs. Why had she left him so abruptly? He'd looked sorry to see her go. It was just such a shock to bump into him like that. She had not taken advantage of the situation.

As Caroline washed her hands in the sink, she stared at her reflection. She looked so wasted. She put on some lipstick which brightened her face. Why couldn't she have bumped into Dr. Pine after she had gone to the washroom? Had Dr. Pine left the restaurant? He didn't have a winter coat on, he might still be there. Was he alone or with his girlfriend?

Caroline rushed up the stairs, anxious to tell Paulina. At their table, she said: "You won't believe who is here, who I talked to. Dr. Pine."

"Oh, I thought you might see him tonight." Paulina acted blasé. "I had a feeling you would but I didn't want to mention it to you."

Caroline wasn't sure if she should believe her sister who thought she was a bit of a psychic.

"Is he still here?" Paulina asked. Caroline looked around the restaurant and saw Dr. Pine alone at a table by an ice-covered window. He was busy eating his meal.
"There, near the window."

Her sister looked over and stared.

"Don't be so obvious," Caroline said.

"Invite him to join us."

"What? I can't do that."

 "Why not?" Paulina challenged her.

"Are you sure it's okay?"

"Sure, ask him to join us. I ordered some dessert so we have to stay anyway."

Caroline got up and went to Dr. Pine's table. When he saw her coming towards him, he looked worried.

"Hi. My sister and I wondered if you would like to join us."

She pointed at the table where Paulina pretended to read the menu.

 "I can't. I'm on call."

Caroline wondered why, if Dr. Pine was on call, he couldn't join them. What difference would it make if he sat at their table rather than this one? She didn't understand doctors' rules and protocol.

"Well, we are leaving soon anyway," Caroline added quickly to save face.

"You must make sure to have your follow-up appointment."

"Yes, I will. Take care."

Caroline noticed there was only a wing left on his plate to eat.

She sat back down at her table.

"He didn't want to join us."

"Ah, well. I knew he wouldn't. Let's just have the dessert and go."

Caroline agreed. She still believed that Dr. Pine cared about her but did he love her? She felt warmth emanate from him, but was it real, or was it fake, like the flames in the restaurant fireplace?

* * *

The cemetery was a short walk from Caroline's new home. She passed the iron gates into the pastoral landscape. She didn't recognize the names carved into the granite and marble monuments but she knew they had meaning to some family. Thomas lay to rest in her family's burial ground.

Caroline wondered which road to take to the grave. All the roads looked the same, lined by century old trees. The last time she'd been here was on the morning of Thomas's burial ceremony. She had come in Paulina's car with their mother. Her father had been unwell and couldn't attend. Caroline missed his presence. Mr. Neufeld had not been able to attend either. As the rain fell heavily, the women held on to their umbrellas while the pastor prayed. Then the urn, a small polished wooden box she'd chosen for the ashes, had been deposited in the wet earth. When they left, their shoes were muddy.

Now the morning was sunny and warm. Caroline went up the steep road toward the cemetery office. From there, she knew she could find the grave. She felt apprehensive about being alone though walking helped her to relax. She loved to take long walks and did so every day.

Arriving at the one story office building, Caroline recognized the road to take. Soon she saw the family monument among the tall leafy trees. She couldn't see anyone at other grave sites. It was eerie. She looked down at the plaque with Thomas's name but felt nothing. She went to her grandmother's grave. Her name was engraved on a small marble headstone. Caroline asked to be forgiven for not having been strong enough to visit her at the hospital in her last hour. At twenty years old, she hadn't been emotionally able to do so. She had grown stronger. She'd sat by Thomas's bed in the ICU and held his thin hand hoping he could feel her love.

She didn't want to be in the cemetery anymore. As she walked back down the road, Caroline realized her visit had not been cathartic. The ashes were there but it meant little since Thomas wasn't there.

* * *

Caroline didn't know where it came from, the sudden irrational urge to go to Mountainside Hospital, but she decided to follow it. Her article could wait, she didn't have a deadline. As she washed her hair in the shower and felt the warm water flow over her body, Caroline guessed that the urge had something to do with having left Thomas there. Did it have to do with the wild hope that she would "see" Thomas again? Did she believe Thomas's "ghost" was in the hospital?

Caroline decided she would go to the hospital library to do some research. She blow-dried her hair and decided to wear a long skirt, a raspberry coloured t-shirt, and her khaki jacket. Wearing favourite clothes made her feel better. She slipped on sandals and then left the apartment after saying goodbye to Mel, who preferred to sleep rather than play all day.

On the bus to the hospital, Caroline looked out the window and thought about how she would have liked to be a nurse but didn't have the stamina for such strenuous work.

"You look like Florence Nightingale," Thomas had remarked once in passing. He'd noticed the photo of the young British heroine on the cover of the biography she was reading. Caroline took it as a compliment. She did have the same round face, round chin. And she had determination though nothing like Nightingale whose care giving spirit still touched every hospital.

Caroline entered Mountainside and headed to the library on the main floor. She pulled the heavy oak door then entered the room where medical journals and magazines were displayed on open shelves. A young doctor in his white lab coat, a stethoscope around his neck, sat in one of the leatherette armchairs, consulting a magazine. Had Dr. Pine been here too? A couple of students at the computers discussed their upcoming exams.

Caroline sat down in an armchair, unable to stretch her legs due to an old battered coffee table heaped with more magazines. After an hour of reading various articles of interest, Caroline felt hungry and decided she would go back home for lunch.

In the corridor, Caroline felt herself swept up in the noon hour rush of medical personnel, visitors, and a few patients pushing their IV poles towards the coffee shop. As she passed the bank of elevators, Caroline looked twice at a stocky man with a deep tan. He had on a bright blue shirt and black pants. He looked at his watch, then impatiently at the elevator doors, then back at his watch. Was it possible? Was that Dr. Pine?

She rushed up behind him and poked his shoulder with her finger, harder than planned. He whipped around to see who had the nerve to do that, but when he saw it was her, his irritation visibly melted.

"Dr. Pine. It's so nice to see you!" She spoke first, and to explain why she was there, she added, "I'm doing research at the library here."

"Mrs. Sauvé." He smiled at her. "I must get back to you about the article. I am very sorry I have been on holiday and now I am pressed for time with work."

"That's fine, whenever you can."

Caroline looked up into his warm brown eyes. So he wanted to work on the article. He had the power to lift her out of mourning.

"I have your phone number. I will call you," Dr. Pine said loudly as if he wanted people around them to take note that he was talking with her.

An elevator door slid open and he went with the crowd towards it. He looked surprised when he turned around and saw she was still where he had left her. Caroline pointed playfully at the exit door to let him know she was leaving the hospital. He appeared disappointed as the elevator door closed. She wished she was on the elevator with him.

Dr. Pine said he would call about the article and that he had her phone number. Had he recorded it in his cell phone? When she was with him, the cells in her body sparkled like bubbles of *rosé* in a glass. She couldn't imagine living, or desiring to be alive, if their connection ever ended. She had to tell someone that she had seen him. Paulina, or Joanie maybe.

As she left the hospital, Caroline felt almost as happy as if she had seen Thomas again.

* * *

The article was finished. Dr. Pine had read the final draft and approved it. Caroline clicked the "send" command on the computer. The file would arrive within seconds in the Inbox of the editor who'd accepted it for publication. She felt a thrill at the thought of the article appearing at last in the pages of the prestigious magazine.

She had never worked as hard on an article. Dr. Pine rarely had time to talk with her. She'd had to give him deadlines, threaten to give up, wait *ad nauseam*. Yet his enthusiasm and praise for each draft she wrote kept her from abandoning the project. Her conversations with him were instructive since she hadn't known much about medicine, or the life of a surgeon. Her admiration increased since he devoted himself to his patients. She couldn't forget how he'd trembled from fatigue, hardly able to get up from his office chair. Yet his work saved lives. He had saved hers. She wouldn't be writing if he had not operated on her so skilfully.

Once he had reached her to announce: "I have twenty minutes free till I operate, so let's do this." She couldn't believe he'd called just before he was due in the operating room. It had made her feel valued. She sensed he was impressed by her professionalism and grateful for her attention. Another time he'd called from the Trudeau Airport. He was on his way to a conference in Boston and had half an hour before his flight. He'd used his cell phone but since she couldn't hear him clearly, he called back on a public pay phone. The image of Dr. Pine standing in the airport answering her questions on the pay phone struck her as funny and sweet.

Once he called her around 10 p.m. from his office. His voice was raspy from a bad cold. After a few minutes, she said gently, "Are you sure you want to go over the article tonight? Shouldn't you get yourself a glass of water or a cough drop?" But he said no, he was fine, and continued the revision between coughing fits.

Caroline stared at her computer screen where there appeared a confirmation that the article was received at the magazine. She knew that, more important than the money, the article would promote Dr. Pine's work and perhaps earn her more love.

HEALING

It was noon. Caroline couldn't concentrate on her work at the computer, troubled by Dr. Pine's call the evening before. She decided to go to Saint-Joseph's Oratory since it was a sunny day and she could enjoy the panoramic view of Montreal. She slipped on her coat, found her bag, and went out.

The air was fresh and cleared her thoughts. Within minutes, she was at the entrance of the Oratory which amazed her. This was a holy site that people travelled from all over the world to visit; people who saved money to come here for worship and healing. Mexicans, Hindus, Japanese, Koreans, Africans, and many other nationalities mingled on top of the mountain with Canadians and Americans. She loved to see how she fit in with everyone and no one stared at her as if she didn't belong.

As Caroline passed under the cement arch onto the grounds, she enjoyed the sudden change in landscape. Flowerbeds lined wide alleys that went up the mountain slope towards the Basilica. The cement staircase was roped off for pilgrims who chose to climb the steps on their knees in prayer, as if they were climbing the stairs to heaven.

Caroline remembered how, as a child in Catholic school, she would come here on field trips with the nuns. On one particular visit, Caroline had been in a lot of pain due to having twisted her ankle the day before but she hadn't told the teacher. Each step had been excruciating. Shy, filled with anxious thoughts about her unpredictable father, she was often ill and missed school. But she liked to study and was first in her class.

Her mother had instructed Paulina and her not to tell anyone that their father had a "drinking problem." She kept the secret though she didn't understand what it meant. She sensed her father's suffering, how he stumbled back to them, often ill, sometimes turning on them with angry words. Yet she loved her father. When she'd limped into the sanctuary behind her teacher and the other girls, she had prayed that Jesus take care of him and heal his pain. At the souvenir shop, she'd purchased with her allowance money, a plastic pink rosary and a picture of Brother André for her mother to make her feel better.

Caroline decided to test her endurance and hike up the mountain rather than take the minibus. She climbed at a slow pace, and when she made it to the top, she breathed in deeply the fresh air. She was ecstatic that her repaired heart tolerated the demanding exercise. The city, the river and the distant shore sparkled before her.

Caroline entered the dark sanctuary and slipped into a pew at the back. Behind the altar, a statue of St-Joseph stood in a halo of golden rays. At the side, a woman held up her hands to touch the pierced feet of Jesus on a tall wooden cross. Head down, long dark hair hiding her face, she was deep in prayer. Caroline was uncomfortable by this display of need but she hoped the woman would experience the relief she sought. A line of people waited behind her.

Caroline's thoughts turned to the phone call she had received from Dr. Pine the evening before.

"I want to thank you very much for the article, Mrs. Sauvé. It's a wonderful thing you did for the foundation, thank you so much."

She wished he would call her Caroline. She'd asked him to but he didn't. And would he ever want her to call him Ken? Perhaps things would change now that the article was published and he was pleased with it.

"I'm happy that you like it. The photo adds a nice touch," she said. The magazine had sent a staff photographer to take a picture of Dr. Pine for the article.

"Well, I didn't have much time to give him. I don't know why you did this for me....."

In the whirl of emotions, Caroline blurted out what she had kept secret: "I love you very much." Her declaration was met with silence.

".....you know I have a girlfriend?"

Yes, she knew he had a girlfriend but he hardly ever mentioned her and she wasn't his wife.

"Why aren't you married?" Her bold question matched her bold emotional statement.

"Well, I'm not sure..." Dr. Pine began, surprised. "I guess we don't have time to get married."

Caroline couldn't believe that was the reason. No time to marry? That seemed shallow.

"Let's be friends, all right?" Dr. Pine offered.

Did she want to accept that? She wanted a lot more but Dr. Pine didn't love her, not as she loved him. She would have to think about this twist in their relationship.

"I don't know. Anyway, thanks for calling."

"Are you going to be okay?" Dr. Pine asked.

"Sure. I'm fine." She wanted to keep a shred of dignity.

The scent of incense and candle wax in the sanctuary reminded Caroline where she was. How naive to think that Dr. Pine would love her back, would want her, rather than his girlfriend. She had made an error. She should not be in love with a man who lived with another woman. Even though he wasn't wearing a ring, he had made a choice. And she didn't want to hurt another woman. Yet she felt so much love for him. Was it love? She missed Thomas. If he were here beside her in the pew, everything would be all right. He knew how to comfort her. He had loved her.

Caroline would light a candle in his memory. She slipped out of the pew and walked to the dark hall with a high-domed ceiling. It reminded her of a medieval crypt. On each side, there were metal stands holding hundreds of votive candles. She headed to the largest stand in the middle of the hall. Another statue of St-Joseph, holding the child Jesus in his arms, stood on a pedestal. People praying were motionless as wax figures.

Her dollar coin rattled loudly in the tin box. She took a bamboo stick and held it to the flame of a candle until it flared up. Then she lit her own candle. Around her, in the flickering dark, there were children grasping their fathers by the hand, mothers pushing strollers, students with backpacks, seniors shuffling, some with canes, and people in wheel chairs. She looked up and saw a macabre collection of ancient wooden crutches hanging from a shelf. These had reputedly been left behind by pilgrims who had been healed at the Oratory. She believed miracles happened but she wasn't sure about all these crutches. Her heart operation had been risky but she had made it up the mountain.

* * *

Caroline liked being in the darkness of the taxicab as it sped along Sherbrooke Street to Jenny and Jonathan's condo. She'd accepted their Christmas dinner invitation. At first, she wanted to refuse since she didn't know if she could bear going without Thomas. But she didn't want to disappoint her friends. They both had given her and Thomas their support through the years of crisis. And she enjoyed their company. Jenny had even hinted there might be someone she'd like to meet; a friend of Jonathan's who had also been invited.

She decided to take a taxi rather than the bus because the weather had turned stormy. She wanted to make sure she arrived at Jenny and Jonathan's looking pretty rather than like a wet cat coming in from the snow. She gripped the door handle as the taxi made a sharp turn onto the street that climbed up to where Jenny and Jonathan lived on the mountain. She paid the cab driver who thanked her for the tip, then drove off.

Caroline stood on the sidewalk before the condo building and watched the snowflakes fall gently, white and pure. There was something cozy about a December snowstorm, something that calmed the nerves of city dwellers since they had to slow their pace in order to stay safe. Caroline walked up the cement steps and rang the doorbell. She heard a man's steps and then the door opened. She felt herself swept up into Jonathan's affectionate hug.

"How lovely it is to see you, Caroline. We are so happy you decided to come."

She entered the sumptuous apartment with glossy pinewood floors. Jenny's taste in winter whites, creams, and beiges was impeccable as a professional decorator's. The happiness this couple felt together suffused the pristine rooms with warmth and made it a real home. Jonathan hung her coat in the hall closet. Caroline took her boots off and slipped into her *pièce de résistance*, her high heels. She could wear the black velvet shoes on a special occasion like this. She had bought them because the shoes made her feel like a Russian princess, the straps accenting her slim ankles. The shoes drew the attention away from her well-worn jean skirt and red sweater. She missed the days when she could buy a new dress for an evening out like this, but she had to be careful since she hadn't earned money lately. Beginning the New Year, she'd work hard as her health improved.

A few people she recognized lounged on the white sofa, and in the set of matching armchairs. She smiled at Karen, a friend of Jenny's whom she felt drawn to since her husband had passed away recently also. Before she could go and sit beside her, Jenny appeared and hugged her. "We are so glad you came tonight!"

Caroline looked at Jenny who glowed from her efforts in the kitchen but also from seeing her. Jenny was petite and dressed impeccably. Her long blond hair curled down her back. Her makeup was applied lightly but enhanced her doll-like features. Caroline remembered how Jenny had visited her in the hospital bringing bouquets of flowers.

She handed Jenny the gift box of white chocolate bark with almonds.

"You really didn't have to, dear."

"It's my pleasure. Thank you for inviting me. It's nice to come here and know I will be spoilt," she added sincerely. Jenny waved her hand lightly, an amused smile on her lips, as if the comment were slightly silly.

"Let's move into the dining room now," Jenny called to everyone in the living-room. Caroline followed her. She marvelled at the perfection of the luxurious dining table setting. She could have been at the Ritz Carlton Hotel yet it had Jenny's trademark home touch. The delicate chandelier with crystal drops sparkled over the long narrow table covered in a white linen tablecloth. There were name tags at each place setting. She found hers and sat down. Patricia was seated across, and a stranger down on her left. She read "Stash" on his name tag. In the living-room, she'd noticed him because of his shiny brown hair that grazed his shoulders. She liked long hair on men.

She smiled at Stash as he made himself comfortable beside her. He wore a grey suit threadbare at the sleeves. He stared at the silver cutlery by his plate. He seemed shy. This made her feel less shy. Stash must be Jonathan's friend who had recently returned to Montreal after living in Toronto for several years.

Maybe it was the romantic lighting of the chandelier, or the rich tasty dish of noodles in cream sauce, but Caroline began to feel attracted to this quiet man. And Stash's eyes feasted on her in between bites of the creamy noodles. The conversation at the table increased in liveliness as Jonathan, a tall man with tall tales, poured the wine in each glass, up to the brim, his booming laughter cheering everyone. Caroline drank her usual Perrier with a lemon slice. The dozen or so men and women around the table were a collection of teachers, writers and photographers, some of whom Caroline had met before. But she wanted to know more about Stash. As the dessert was served, a delectable slice of strawberry cheesecake, she asked him a personal question: "Do you work with Jonathan at the university?"

"No," Stash answered. He smiled at her, obviously glad she'd broken the silence. "No, I just came back from Toronto and I'm looking for work."

"Where did you work in Toronto?"

"The last job was at a magazine."

Stash named the magazine which was reputable. Caroline perked up. This was the world she knew. "Are you a writer?" Stash looked down at the piece of cheesecake on his fork. "Well, no. I worked more in the editorial department." This was intriguing but Caroline sensed that Stash didn't want to talk about it so didn't press him. She did want to ask him about his name.

"Is Stash a nickname?"

"It's short for Stanislav. My parents have roots in Ukraine."

"That's interesting."

He asked her what she did and when she told him that she was a freelance writer, she could tell he was impressed.

The meal ended and the guests returned to the living-room. Caroline rested on the sofa and Stash came to sit beside her. She felt exhausted by now and thought it was time for her to go home. It was past ten p.m. She was usually getting ready for bed by that time. She would be the first to leave but she knew that Jenny and Jonathan would understand. They were familiar with her fragile health. What would Stash think if he knew what she had been through? She excused herself and went to find Jenny who was in the dining room removing the last dishes.

"Jenny, it's been lovely but I have to go. I am so sorry to be the first but you know how I am unable to stay up late." Her host looked tired also. She had refused Caroline's offer to clear the table or do the dishes. Jonathan would help her. "Sure, we understand. Thanks so much for coming. I'll call a taxi for you?"

Caroline went back into the living room to say goodbye to a few people including Stash. He accompanied her to the entry hall where he helped her slip on her coat. "I'm sorry I don't have a car at this time. I would have liked to drive you home."

"Thanks. No problem."

Caroline thought that was nice of Stash to be honest about his situation. He asked for her phone number and she wrote it down on a piece of paper he'd found in his pocket. He invited to take her out for a coffee and she agreed. He left quietly when Jenny came to say the taxi was on its way and she'd wait with her.

"No, it's not necessary. You must get back to your guests. Say goodbye to Jonathan for me please." They hugged then Caroline was alone. She slipped off her high heels, put them in the bag and then tugged on her boots, all the while wondering if she really wanted to see Stash again? Maybe he wouldn't call her.

An hour later, she was in her apartment dressed in her long-sleeved nightgown. Mel was lying on the carpet by the bed. She bent down and petted his furry head and scratched behind his ears. He started to purr. No doubt he'd missed her as he wasn't used to her going out in the evening, or at all.

* * *

At the bookstore café, Caroline could barely recognize Stash. Was this the same man she had been attracted to a week ago at Jenny and Jonathan's? He stood up from the table and waved at her. His long brown hair was now cut chin length. Why had he done that? Did he think she preferred short hair? Stash had a nice face but he no longer looked romantic. His faded blue jeans were held up by a tattered belt. His scuffed leather jacket revealed a red t-shirt that had turned pink from too many washes. Who was this man? Caroline was glad she agreed to meet him only for a cup of coffee. He greeted her with wide eyes as if she were a famous actress. And she did have to use acting skills, so taken aback by his different appearance. She joined him at the small round table.

"What can I get for you Caroline?"

She was touched that Stash wanted to treat her so she asked for an English Breakfast tea. After trying various flavoured and herbal teas including green tea which upset her stomach, she now only liked black tea.

"Sure, I'll be right back. Do you want sugar and milk?"

"No, just plain, thanks."

Caroline watched this stranger go up to the counter. She didn't want to stare so she looked around the café which was just a small area in a large chain bookstore. The half-dozen tables were all taken by people drinking coffee or tea, some reading magazines or books borrowed from the store shelves. The hot beverage should calm her butterflies, Caroline thought, as Stash deposited the extra large ceramic cup in front of her. It was odd how the round table was made only big enough to accommodate two mugs but she kept this observation to herself. Stash stirred milk into his coffee. Caroline wanted to know more about his past.

"How long did you work at the publishing house in Toronto?"

"I worked there for about five years. I got tired of being in sales though."

"I thought you said you worked in the editorial department?".

"Oh, I did some editing but it wasn't that often."

Stash's vague answer left Caroline feeling confused. Hadn't he said at the dinner party that he did editing? He hadn't mentioned sales before. So did this mean he was really a sales rep who did some editing on the side, if even that? Stash might have said he was an editor just to impress her. He didn't seem to want to pursue the topic of his work and bent his head closer to hers.

"So how long have you been alone?" he asked.

"My husband passed away three years ago," Caroline answered, more sharply than she intended. The bald question increased her mistrust. Stash came with a good reference. He was a friend of Jonathan's, yet she felt that he wasn't like Jonathan at all. In fact, now his name recalled her days as a hippie when the word "stash" referred to drugs. She had become conservative and frowned on drugs.

"I'm sorry to hear that. I've never experienced such a loss." His sympathetic words made her feel a little better.

"Well, we were very close. We were married for more than twenty years."

"I've never been married."

"Oh, you never met someone you wanted to marry?" She knew this might be a bit nosy but she wanted to find out where Stash stood in his love life.

"Well, there was a woman I lived with who I wanted to marry but she didn't want to marry me. And she ended up leaving me suddenly for another man."

"I am sorry for you."

She truly was. She saw that Stash was saddened by this memory. He told her he'd returned to Montreal to be near his elderly mother who needed his help. The noise in the café was increasing as more people came in for a mid-afternoon treat. Caroline was tired but Stash wanted to prolong the date.

"Would you like another cup of tea? Or do you want to go look at the books?"

. "No, thank you very much." Caroline answered simply. She knew there was not a spark between them. Whatever had attracted her to Stash at the dinner party had been ephemeral but Stash seemed to like her even more which made her nervous. She reached for her coat on the back of her chair. She slipped on one sleeve then the other: "Excuse me but I really need to get back home. I feel exhausted. I hope I'm not coming down with something."

"Oh, that's too bad. Maybe we can come back here soon and buy some books."

She didn't want to commit to this but nodded. Stash zipped up his jacket. They were out of the bookstore and on Ste -Catherine Street.

"I wish I had a car." Stash seemed distraught. "I plan to buy one as soon as I find work here. Then I can drive you home."

"Oh, don't worry. It's easy for me to get home by bus."

She knew he lived somewhere in Montreal West which was in a totally different direction. He walked with her to the bus stop. The afternoon air was cold, crisp and hard to breathe in. They didn't have to chat long as the bus pulled up. She got in line, Stash sticking next to her until they reached the open door. "I'll call you soon," Stash said, then bent down and kissed her on the mouth.

Caroline climbed the steps into the bus and the driver shut the door behind her. Stash stared through the window with a smug look. She could still feel the pressure of his kiss as she paid her fare and then found her way to the back where there was an empty seat. She

114

pulled a tissue from her bag and wiped her lips. She felt disgusted by Stash's impudence. Was she turning into a nun?

At her building, Caroline unlocked the two bolts on her door, then without even taking her boots off, rushed into the bathroom to rinse her mouth. The cat watched her movements with wide curious eyes.

She removed her coat and boots and petted Mel who followed her into the kitchenette. His bowl was empty so she added some food bits. She needed tea to warm up so she filled the kettle and plugged it into the wall. Soon, holding her steaming cup of tea, Caroline returned to the living-room where her gaze fell on Thomas's painting. She'd hung it above the sofa bed in a prominent place. Again, she felt strengthened by the image of the dancing woman with sad eyes.

This apartment was her home now. She didn't want to think about Stash. She didn't want to think about Dr. Pine. She had her memories of Thomas's love. Her writing projects gave her a reason to get out of bed in the morning. Caroline sat down in front of the computer and switched it on. Mel rubbed against her leg. She bent down to pat his soft fur. Then she began to type ideas and notes that were tumbling out for a new article.

About the Author

Anne Cimon was born in Montreal, Quebec. She enjoys writing her stories, poetry, and articles in long hand, sitting in her wing chair. Now she lives near the river outside of Montreal.